JOHN PAUL'S ROCK

By
Frank Parker Day

Drawings by
Mabel K. Day

First Published in 1932.

Stillwoods Edition

Stillwoods.Blogspot.Ca

Catalogue Information:
Title: John Paul's Rock
Author: Frank Parker Day (1881-1950)
Illustrated by: Mabel K. Day
First Published by: Minton, Balch & Company, New York 1932.
This Edition by: Stillwoods, 2021, (Doug Frizzle)
ISBN Canada: 978-1-989788-28-8
Blog: Stillwoods.Blogspot.Ca
Storefront: http://www.lulu.com/spotlight/lulubook22

Keywords: John Paul's Rock, Frank Parker Day, Mi'kmaq, Nova Scotia

Notes:
In all probability much of the Mi'kmaq lore in this story comes from Day's friend and guide, Jim Charles.

Cautionary Note: Books by Stillwoods are intended to make old stories available to readers, collectors and researchers. The editor, or rather digitizer has not altered the original publication.

This story may contain language and racial terms that are not appropriate to today. I apologize for them; I know that the author was using his voice to excite, entertain and educate his audience. This work was published almost 90 years ago.

I hope you enjoy and share this story; I have.
Doug Frizzle

This Stillwoods edition is dedicated to the Phinney Family, explicitly Horton, Norman and Roger Phinney. Through them I learned to love Kedge —now a National Park.

Author Dedication: To the Faculty and Undergraduates of Union College

No reference is intended in this book to any actual character or definite district.

CONTENTS

The Rock

I THE ROCK

On a hillside, in the very interior of Nova Scotia, is a towering grey Rock, patriarch of a thousand lesser rocks scattered along the ancient glacier's trail. Grim it stands, defiant of time or fate. Ages past, it sprang full-grown through an earth rift from the boiling magma below; ages past, it left the howling north, to travel southward with slow dignity, set like a precious stone in a mountain of crystal. A thousand years it rode its glittering chariot, till the sun's heat turned the ice mountain into green rivers roaring and swirling to the sea. Then the Rock settled majestically and drove its foundations deep into the Nova Scotia hillside, to await with indifference the next revolution of nature. To it a thousand years are but a day; the impertinent animal, man, a newcomer. Wind-driven rain has pelted it through the centuries, envious frosts have rent spawls and slivers from its base, earthquakes have jostled it, but still its lichen-covered bulk towers toward sun and stars, calm, unmoved, majestic.

About the Rock is a land of silence, broken only in seasons by the chatter of ducks upon the lake, by the plaintive love-call of the moose, by the snap of a dried twig beneath the foot of some wild thing, by the splash of a rising trout or the gossip of yellow reeds, by the winter challenge that wind-swept spruces fling to arrogant hemlocks.

East and west a great lake stretches before it, eastern and western shores lost in mist and distance; northward, facing the Rock's steep side, are many smaller lakes with connecting streams and stillwaters, bogs clad in hardhacks and blueberry bushes and dotted with spindly hackmatacks, and miles upon miles of forest, spruce and fir evergreens in the lowlands and hardwoods upon the ridged uplands; southward, behind the Rock, the land rises into forested hills from which a broad swift brook curves into the lake. Virgin forests guard rear and flanks. Out upon the lake, the easy way of approach, the great Rock keeps stern watch. Adventurous sportsmen, prospectors far afield in search of gold, lumbermen cruising new timber limits use the Rock as a guiding mark, and call it John Paul's Rock, for so it was named on the map by a stooped, grey-headed white man, though few know why it is so called, nor how John Paul achieved a cenotaph grander and more enduring than that of kings and emperors.

Salmon at The Forks

In early June of John Paul's twenty-first year, he was salmon fishing at the Forks with Lawyer Freeman and his two boys, Alan and David. Both boys had learned to catch trout under John Paul's instruction—he had been guide for the Freeman family since he was a boy of fifteen—but this was the first trial for salmon on the big river. John Paul and Alan Freeman, aged sixteen, were in the canoe that was anchored by the stern and yawed to and fro in the swift current; John Paul sat on the bottom amidships, Alan on the bow seat. On the nearby sand-bar below the old buttress with Lawyer Freeman was David, aged twelve, watching the water for a rising fish and eagerly awaiting his turn. John Paul in the canoe gave his instructions with a minimum of words:

"Tie on number four Black Dose. Short line first. Fish each side of canoe, current carry down fly. Let out foot of line every second cast. If he come don't strike like for trout, pull slow. Fish slow for salmon, quick for trout."

It was a glorious morning. The sun touched the green wooded hills half way down, the valleys were in shadow and lazy rising mists. At the Forks, two swirling rivers from the hills met to form a calm deep pool, a favourite place for resting or spawning salmon. The water was emerald green, ice-cold and crystal clear, the bottom a medley of small worn quartz stones white, yellow, and red. To glance over the canoe's gunwale filled one with a desire to plunge in. The morning, the hills bathed in sunshine, the green rushing river, the banks gay with laurel and Indian Arrow; a fisherman's dream of heaven.

Presently a fish came short.

"Reel up quick; rest him ten minutes," said John Paul. The handsome, self-willed Alan was loath to obey but John Paul was insistent.

"Reel up quick or he no come again."

Alan obeyed scowling. John Paul lit his pipe and sat still and unimpressed as a Chinese idol. Through ten minutes that seemed an age, Alan fidgeted on the bow seat. David danced on the sand-bar, and showered questions upon his indulgent father.

"Swing back cast; change number four to number six," said John Paul.

3

When the long ten minutes were up, John Paul allowed his pupil to begin again, and cast from side to side with a short line that the current swept down in a swift arc. Little by little the line was lengthened till the Black Dose swung over the nose of the salmon, that lay behind a rock, his belly touching the multi-coloured pebbles. The big fish rose savagely with a great splash, took the fly to the bottom, and was hooked before Alan realized what had happened.

"Reel in; keep tight line.

"Look out for first jump.

"Let reel free and lower tip quick when he quiver and run for jump."

John Paul raised himself with a hand on either gunwale, stepped lightly astern, pulled the anchor, and with a deft twist of the paddle turned the canoe's bow to the sand-bar. He beached the canoe, keeping an eye upon Alan, and steadied the canoe as Alan stepped out, his hand upon the reel, his eye upon the line.

"Look out for first jump.

"There he go; slack line, down tip."

Alan's face was hot and flushed; in Lawyer Freeman's eyes was a strange gleam; David hopped on the sand-bar and shouted in ecstasy; John Paul stood still and calm, puffing slowly at his pipe.

At the Forks, the main river rushes by buttress and sand-bar, and spends its force in the big pool. Close to the sand-bar, inside the current, is a dead-water and into this John Paul urged Alan to draw the hooked salmon, so that the light leader would not have to bear the weight of both fish and current. Three times the salmon sprang into the air, a glittering bow of silver; three times in answer to John Paul's shout Alan slackened his line and dipped his rod's tip. Presently the fish tired and was drawn into the dead-water. Showing a gleaming side, he came close to the sand-bar. John Paul took the net and, standing firm on the river's brink, scooped him out to thump and gleam among the grasses. Alan, flushed and radiant with his first salmon, stepped forward and patted John Paul's shoulder.

"Thanks, John Paul, you're a brick."

"Good fish," replied John Paul laconically, "him weigh seventeen pound."

Now it was David's turn though Alan pouted and wanted to fish again. There were plenty of rising fish in the river. David hooked a fish, lost him on the first jump, hooked another fifty yards down in the

4

current, and in twenty minutes John Paul had scooped him out to thump beside Alan's on the bank.

Lunch on the sand-bar, high noon, two glittering fish in the grasses, sunshine flooding wooded valleys, the green river rushing by in swirls and eddies of foam and bubbles, two happy boys with a day in their hearts never to be forgotten.

John Paul made a small fire between two stones, rigged a pot-stick, boiled the kettle and threw in the tea to steep. Brook trout were in the pan, bacon fat sizzling on their brown skins; there were mugs of hot tea and piles of buttered bread with strawberry jam and oranges. Everything was as it should be; only once in a while in life come such moments.

After lunch, John Paul and Lawyer Freeman lit their pipes and settled themselves in sand and grass. David nestled against his father's thigh; Alan sat erect, staring at the river and watching for another rising fish.

"Wouldn't it be fine, Dad," said little David suddenly, "if John Paul were our brother?"

Alan laughed lightly; "David makes such silly remarks," he said in his elder brother manner. Lawyer Freeman smiled indulgently at the warm bright face pressed against his leg. John Paul puffed evenly on his pipe, and neither spoke nor moved his head; you might have said that he had not even heard David's remark. But he had heard and he never forgot.

"Tell us a story, John Paul," said David. "Tell us a story about the old Micmacs."

"Me no story-teller," replied John Paul. "Me guide, hunter, fisherman, trapper."

"Tell us about the Indian Mound you showed us today," insisted David.

"Old Micmacs come there to make spear-heads, arrow-heads. You see flint chips all over ground. Chip with drops of cold water on hot stone. No flint there, carry flint maybe hundred miles. Pick out high ground near salmon pool. Spear them nights with flares. Spring and summer camp, move to hunting ground fall and winter."

John Paul knew a great deal about the life of the early Micmacs; perhaps if he had been alone with David, he might have told a story full of Indian jokes, but he was shy in the presence of Lawyer Freeman and stuck to a bare recital of facts.

5

A long time they lay drowsily watching the river and listening to its music, till on a signal from Lawyer Freeman John Paul picked up rods and gear and launched the canoe for the long homeward journey.

"What a happy day, Dad!" said little David. "You are good to us; we can never be so happy again."

They glided off on the green water, the multicoloured pebbles rushing at the bow. They swept round the curve by the wooded island. The yellow sand-bar in the sunshine was deserted, and the ripple on the bar sang in a strange minor key.

John Paul

At the age of twenty-five, John Paul was living in a neat cabin that he had inherited from his father, former chief of the Indians on the reserve at Mooin River. Full grown, he was tall and erect, slim of leg but deep-chested and broad of shoulder, for never in his life had he walked when he could travel by canoe. The canoe was to him what the horse is to the Westerner, or the automobile to the city-dweller; and in his land of lake, still-water and river, he could cover hundreds of miles with few portages which were, for the most part, easy carries. His face was broad and bronzed, with the high Mongolian cheek bone, and something of the inscrutability of the Orient. His charm was in an infrequent but wistful and melancholy smile that revealed strong regular teeth and almost closed his slitty eyes. Brown, courageous, truthful eyes they were, quick and alert, that saw everything upon the ground, everything that moved on the hillside, every cloud that puffed across the blue. His clothing, not in the least professional, consisted of any slouch hat, coat, sweater, trousers that he could get.

He was a good-natured easy-going stoic and fatalist. From childhood he had lived on the reserve allotted to the Indians by the whites, and he had seen his tribe die swiftly of drink and consumption. Yet he spent no time in mourning over his vanishing race, nor in reviling the greed of white men. He despised those professional Indians who snivelled over their fate and were full of pretended regrets for the past. He knew that Force was the Ultimate Right, and he and his friend Joe Meuse had long since decided that Indian rights were a thing of naught, that Indians must make the best of the conditions in which they found themselves and get what they could. Of course he could not shake off his origin, his racial characteristics or his memories; for sometimes when he woke at night, strange tags of Micmac legends went buzzing through his brain. These he dismissed as idle fancies. He knew without sadness that he was almost the last of a race, choked by a stronger and more practical civilization, and that in another generation the Micmacs would be gone.

He was much sought after as a guide, for he was a strong and tireless hunter; none could pole a canoe more swiftly up a rapid, make camp more quickly, or sound a more plaintive and seductive call on the birch horn. He never left knives or hatchets lying behind when he broke camp, nor stole much, nor made a row when drunk. Green hunting parties found him invaluable—to cook and cut wood, to carry canoe and dunnage over rough portages, to lure the moose from the wooded ridge to the open bog, and to keep them out of danger. For all these qualities, he was named by the whites a good Indian.

In his heart, John Paul was indifferent to and rather scornful of most white men. They had none of the qualities that he admired and understood. They were easily excited and shot wildly, they had no sense of balance in a canoe, they were easily lost in the woods, having marked the individual character of neither ridge, stream nor bog, whereas he and Joe Meuse could direct one another to far distant points by telling of the kinds of trees, shapes or rock or ridge, colour of brook or still-water as if they were numbered houses in city blocks. Once in a while there was a spare keen-eyed hunter among the whites who sensed the woods and had the homing instinct; but for the most part he found them soft, fat men, who tired easily, and who made a week of hunting an excuse for a week of drunkenness. Scornfully he used to kick the feet of such, in his effort to waken them, as they lay snoring open-mouthed through the hour before dawn, the best time for calling; and getting no response but a muttered curse, would take his rifle and go out to the bog alone. There he shot the love-sick bull, whose mounted head hung later in the white man's den, a starting point for a lifetime of lying. He sometimes wondered how such soft men had conquered the old Indians and taken all their land.

Autumn, when he guided the moose hunters, was his great season; in winter he trapped mink, fox and otter and fashioned axe and pick handles of straight grained ash wood; in early spring he drove logs on the Sissiboo River; in late spring and summer, he took Lawyer Freeman and his boys trout and salmon fishing, made baskets of bright coloured spruce strips, or wove dainty jewel boxes of sweet hay, though that was really squaw's work. John Paul got a good deal of joy out of the making of baskets; he liked the feel of swamp maple as he tore it into thin strips, the smooth texture of ash wood, the amiable quality of beech, that allowed itself to be worked easily, the rugged toughness of yellow birch. Rock maple with its sullen twists and slivers he disliked.

The unconscious artist within him was pleased with his basket creations; new forms and strange new shapes attracted him; he liked to make creels that hung lightly from the shoulder, and great guides' baskets that distributed the weight evenly and fitted snugly into the small of the back. Innately he liked certain colours, and these he wrought into many combinations for women's baskets. Sometimes, when alone, he paused and smiled wistfully at the work of his hands. Like all artists, he was essentially truthful. He refused to become a professional Indian. Once an inquisitive stranger—for many gaping tourists came to watch John Paul at work—asked him how he got such wonderful colours on his spruce strips, expecting a tale of strange juices extracted from forest plants. John Paul answered simply, "Diamond Dyes," without looking up or pausing in his work.

It was through the weaving of sweet hay baskets that John Paul first noticed Mary Barriyo, daughter of Michael Barriyo, chief of the reserve. For Mary could make strange patterns of porcupine quills upon birchbark boxes, and weave tiny sweet hay jewel baskets more cunningly than he; and John did not like the idea of being excelled in basketry by anyone, especially by a woman. He often visited the Barriyo cabin to look upon her work, and from the work, his eyes gradually travelled to the worker. Mary was good to look upon, and clean and neat in her dress. She kept her father's cabin well, for she had been housemaid for a time in Lawyer Freeman's green-shuttered house in the village, where she had learned something of the art of housekeeping and found favour in the eyes of the whites. John's envy and admiration of her work became a source of desire, that grew as he looked into Mary's shy eyes.

One day as he left the cabin John Paul tossed a spruce twig in her lap. Mary knew what that meant, she was not unwilling and laughed yes at him with her eyes. Their love was as simple as that of the moose in the forest. Old Mike Barriyo gave his consent by his silence—he had a squaw and other girls to work—he had eaten many a deer steak and fat spring salmon that John Paul had killed. John Paul was a good hunter, now he would eat more of his new son's game. In the spring John Paul asked the priest to marry them, and Mary came to his cabin.

Since they satisfied one another, they were happy in their simple way. Mary swept the cabin clean; she could bake light crusty bread and fry a trout to a golden brown. She was not lazy; all day long her slender brown fingers flashed in and out of the basket web she wove. She smiled upon John Paul when he returned from hunting; John Paul loved her and was proud of his squaw.

The future seemed bright and secure; he had Mary, his heart's desire, as wife, Joe Meuse as trusted comrade, and Lawyer Freeman, the great man of the village, as friend.

White Man's Law

In the September of his twenty-seventh year, two years after his marriage, John Paul was guiding a party of moose hunters on the shores of Spar Lake, when one of them was taken seriously ill. They had left him sleeping, when they went out to the bog to call, and on their return found him groaning in the tent, and complaining of a sharp pain in his right groin. His friends whispered appendicitis, and demanded a swift return to the village. John Paul broke camp swiftly, put dunnage and rifles aboard, and pushed out into the lake. One of the whites swung the bow paddle awkwardly; another was seated amidships, holding on his knee the head of the sick man, who lay groaning under the amidship thwart; John Paul was astern. Spar Lake was soon left behind; they threaded two winding still-waters, passed through two little lakes and emerged into Big Mulgrave. Here a stiff southwest wind headed them.

John Paul's stern paddle made vicious swirls and streaks of foam; but the awkward white in the bow gave little aid, and their progress was slow. John hugged the wooded western shore, taking advantage of every promontory, but before they reached the outlet that formed the East Branch, he had wished many times that he had Joe Meuse with him at bow paddle. Though John had made his canoe hump-backed, that is with a rising gunwale amidships after the fashion of the old Micmacs, they shipped the tops of many waves. It was necessary to stop and bale, and the clothing of the sick man was soaked.

There had been heavy rains in early September; Big Mulgrave was brimming full and the East Branch was a flood. John Paul decided to abandon all the portages he usually made with hunters on the East Branch—he could not afford to have a white man die on his hands—and to run every white water including the Bad Falls. He had done it once before with Joe, but it was a big risk with an awkward white in the bow. For John Paul understood what the white did not, that there is no harm in the swirl and foam; the danger lies in the granite claw ten feet above it in the raging torrent. Twice as they flashed through the rapids, came the scrape of canvas upon granite, twice John's heart was in his mouth. The whites were too ignorant to sense the danger. But the touched stones were smooth granite, worn by rushing water, and slicked with river moss; ribs and timbers bent

11

but there was no rip of canvas.

In safety they reached tidewater at the top of the flood just as the sun was sinking. With a sigh of relief, John beached the canoe above the iron highway bridge, and while one of the whites went in search of a doctor, he helped carry the sick man and their belongings to the village inn. He returned after he had done all he could, dragged his canoe above high water mark, turned her bottom up on the river bank, and with dunnage and rifle on shoulder walked homeward along the river trail of the West Branch, just as dusk was falling.

Far off he saw a speck of light twinkling in his cabin window; Mary would be glad to see him unexpected and would have the kettle boiling in a jiffy. As he trudged nearer he was surprised to see the light go out. He came close to his cabin, and guided by the instinct of his race, stepped softly to the window and peeped in cautiously before opening the door. In the dim half-light cast by the fire he saw Mary, his squaw, in the arms of a white man. Anger thumped in his heart and flooded his brain; fierce indignation overcame his usual placid endurance; the whites had taken everything, now even his wife; that he would not bear in patience. In that moment John Paul, a changed man, had a vision of Micmac braves in the war dance; he became the avenger of centuries of injustice to his almost vanished race. Quietly he eased the dunnage bags to the ground, slipped the rifle strap from his shoulder there was a cartridge in the breech, he knew and with one lunge of his shoulder, burst open the bolted door. With a snarl of alarm the young white sprang to his feet; John Paul raised his rifle and shot him through the heart. The white man took a step forward, wavered, crumpled, and fell with open mouth and staring eyes upon the floor. The cabin was full of acrid smoke. Mary sat upon the bed's edge, terror in her downcast eyes; she dared neither to look at John Paul nor to speak to him and cry for mercy; she expected to be shot as soon as John threw another cartridge into the chamber.

But John Paul paid no heed to her; instead, he stepped outside his cabin and listened intently for three or four minutes. No one was on the river trail within sight or sound, a thick patch of scrub spruce lay between his cabin and the next, a hundred yards distant, and he knew that a report within doors would not carry far. When he had satisfied himself that no one had heard the shot, he re-entered his cabin, and turning the dead man over, struck a match and looked at his face. It was as he had anticipated, Alan Freeman, drunken, ne'er-do-well son of Lawyer Freeman, in whose home Mary had served as a maid. The boy he had guided and taught to fish, grown to a man, had paid him ill. He uttered no word, but snuffing out the match with thumb and finger, stooped deliberately, put his strong arms around the body, and slung it over his shoulder. The body, lately so full of life and passion, hung limp as a sack of meal, the legs and arms dangling foolishly. John Paul walked with his burden to the head of the West Branch rapid, just above tidewater, where he had hooked many a grilse and salmon, and wading to his waist, cast the body into the fiercest swirl. It was the beginning of the ebb, he knew the river freed by the outgoing tide would run like a mill-race in the narrow estuary, and with luck, the body would be well out in the Basin by morning, battered beyond recognition by fierce current against sharp rock in the long white-water. He watched the dark form bob off in the white foam of the sinister current, then turned homeward, re-entered the cabin, and sat down to think.

He paid no heed to Mary, still seated upon the bed, and in truth, though she had betrayed him he felt no great anger against her. He had none of the white man's chivalrous attitude towards woman, nor any of their romantic ideas of sex and virtue, but in his heart there was a deeper thought—that women were the helpless prize of the victor. His fathers before him had stolen women from the feckless Malecites, along the St. John River, or even crossed the sea from Cape North to Point au Basques to prey upon Montagnais or Red Indians and bring home canoe loads of captured girls; and these, the legends ran, had quickly fitted themselves to their new masters. No, he was hardly angry with Mary; perhaps she had acted willingly, perhaps half through force. What chance had a poor Indian girl against a handsome insistent white with a gift in his hand! For the moment he hated the whole white race, that had trampled out his people. He was glad he had shot and killed Alan Freeman, and felt that in the eyes of true men he had done what was right. There were plenty of free white girls that Alan could have amused himself with; why had he taken his wife, a poor Indian girl?

Then, as action and introspection were over, and hot anger had faded, a great terror crept into John Paul's mind and obsessed him, a black terror that shrouded his spirit. John Paul, courageous by nature, was sincerely afraid of one thing, *white man's law;* white man's law that reached out mysteriously and took you wherever you were, and shut you up forever in a prison house, or strung you up by the neck on a wooden gallows in the court house square. He had seen Louis LeBlanc hanged for the murder of that Caplan girl, and with the vividness of terror, he recalled the whole dreadful scene: the frightened helpless man that the sheriff half carried to the scaffold, the black cap pulled over the eyes, the solemn prayer of the priest, the sheriff's awful words, the cutting of the rope, the jerk, the dangling figure with twitching legs. He trembled from head to foot; he must run no risk of that, if he had to flee to the ends of the earth.

But where should he turn, whither should he go? He buried his face in his hands and tried to think of a sure way of escape. He could expect no leniency or even justice; he had killed a white man, and no insignificant white but the son of a great man, the representative of white man's law in the whole district. If caught, he must either die on the gallows or spend his whole life in the pen, and never see again the green woods, the brown streams, and flashing white-waters. "Muntu help me," cried an atavistic instinct; then for no apparent reason, but as if by magic, a phrase he had heard from the priest came into his mind: "A great rock in a weary land." He repeated it over and over: "A great rock in a weary land, A great rock in a weary land."

Suddenly an idea full-grown leaped into his terror-ridden mind; he would go to the great Rock in the wilderness and live on it for ever; no one could capture him there, for he could watch their coming and hide, till their departure, in the limitless forest. He sprang up, once more a man of action.

He passed close by Mary, who shrank away, took from the walls two big canvas dunnage sacks, and began to select the things he would take with him. Things must be well considered, and of real value, when a man packs for a lifetime, and carries all on his back. He took rifle, shotgun and ammunition, rods, gaff, and fishing gear, a light axe and hunting knife, a stout square of canvas, a bundle of steel traps and a dozen coils of fox wire, a sheepskin, a wool blanket, a thick shirt, a rubber coat some sportsman had given him, two tried and blackened firepots, all the matches he could find in the cabin, bacon, tobacco, tea, bread, and a sack of flour. It was lucky he had laid in large stores for the hunting season. Last of all he picked up a package of flat files, and weighed them in his hand. He was so confident of his safe escape, now that his plan of action was established, that he stood for a moment looking at the files and smiling scornfully. White men were clever but curiously dishonest; they put poor steel into bright handsome knives, that lost their edges in no time; if an Indian wanted a good basket knife that would hold an edge, he had to buy something that was not a knife at all, but a flat file, and grind it down to a cutting edge.

Somehow in two loads he contrived to back all these possessions to his second canoe on the upper still-water. He overturned and launched his canoe and stowed all in bow and amidships, so that she would trim well with his weight in the stern. Returning to his cabin for the last time, he fumbled in a bankside till he found a piece of soft red sandstone. He re-entered and, going to the dim light of the window, took up a hammer. From the corner of his eye, he watched Mary; she sat trembling, expecting to be battered with stone and hammer. He chipped and hammered till the stone took the form of a rough pyramid, flattened and hollowed on top, pitched steeply on one side and sloping gradually on the other two sides. He struck a match and looked his work over with a squinting craftman's eye; it would serve; Joe Meuse would understand. He stuck it beneath the bed, saying to Mary, "Give Joe Meuse when he come"; and went out into the night without another word.

When he stepped into his canoe and slipped silently down the still-water in the black shadow of the bushes, black terror again fell upon his heart. He was fleeing White Man's Law; perhaps Lawyer Freeman would miss Alan that very night, and begin a search; even now the pursuit might be on. What a fool he had been to dawdle so long about his cabin. He paddled fiercely, drawing out his paddle with a suck, like the ripple of a strong stream about a rock. For an Indian to kill a white man was a fearful crime, and the whole countryside would be aroused and up against him. He was sure that Mary would not tell; an Indian can keep a secret. Dogs could follow his scent only as far as the upper still-water. But from there they might push on with two paddlers in a light canoe. He bent to his paddle. Brambles and thorns that caught at his sleeves seemed fingers of avenging law reaching out to grasp him, clutching at him in the night; a drooping alder struck him a sharp blow across the throat, and again he saw the twitching figure of Louis LeBlanc, and felt the hemp tighten about his own throat. A dark sinister form straddled the sternpost of his canoe, and trailing feet in the water hindered his progress. He dared not look behind. The canoe had no life in her; perhaps he was not moving at all; white man's law had anchored him to the bottom by magic, and when day came, he would still be paddling by the landing place in the upper still-water, and the sheriff and Lawyer Freeman would leap out upon him. Well, he could die; they would never take him living to pen him in a prison house, or string him up by the neck. With that thought his mind was for a moment easier; 'twas but child's talk to say that he was not moving, he could see the alder clumps slipping by him, and he recognized an old pine stub on the southern bank far from the landing place. But his peace of mind lasted but for a moment; an old duck and her flock rose from the reeds with a sudden splash; a moose blundered through a tributary stream, crashing the alders with angry snorts. At these familiar, yet unexpected sounds, his heart thumped in his throat; the inescapable magic of Law was again upon him.

The farther he went, the faster he travelled. He had three long portages to make, and over each three journeys—one with the canoe, two with the dunnage. Over the last of these, he ran. The moon rose in the southeast and plunged into an ink-black cloud; rain pelted against his face; a leaden dawn began to glimmer along the horizon. He paddled on without rest, without food or drink; terror taught him to do things superhuman. By noon he was upon the great lake where he could see far off the giant Rock silhouetted against the sky. With his goal in sight he paddled even more fiercely, foam in every paddle's swirl. A strong wind blew down the lake against him and the blue was lined with whitecaps; he was almost safe when he felt a great weariness come over him. The forced journey down Mulgrave the day before would have worn out most men.

Half delirious with fatigue, he bent to his paddle in one great effort. Heroic figures of Indian braves stepped from island to island; a bright red panther sprawled across the sky, and he felt its fetid breath and rough wet tongue upon his cheek. Surely he could go no farther. Law would get him!

Still he struggled on, and just as the sun touched the tops of the spruces, his canoe nosed into the reeds on the shore before his Rock. He threw down the paddle, leaped out, drew the canoe into hiding, and ran up the slope towards the Rock, holding out both his hands, chanting crazily half-remembered, half-understood words of his native Micmac. He was a worshipper; it was his great Rock in a weary land, that Muntu had prepared for him from the beginning. He was safe; no one could take him there; the magic of the Law was

16

broken in the shadow of the great Rock, older and wiser than white men. He threw himself in the tall grasses at its base, his heart full of peace and thankfulness, and slept, his back pressed tightly against his protector. About midnight a black bear shambled silently out of the forest, sniffed at the sleeping man, and went his way.

The Search

In the morning the village was astir over the disappearance of Alan Freeman, for village news travels fast. His bed had not been slept in, he was nowhere to be found, no one had seen him since late afternoon. His father treated the matter lightly; Alan and he had quarrelled over matters of money and whether Alan should get to work. He loved the boy but was very unhappy in his presence. A bad penny always turns up, he said to himself. By noon after he and David had searched village and wharves and telephoned Digby and Annapolis and other nearby villages, the old man was frankly worried. Alan drank hard, but he could not sleep all day in the woods. The alarm became general; passing ox-teams stopped to pass the news before they lumbered up the heavy hill from the bridge; and before nightfall, tired men had told the story of Alan Freeman's disappearance to groups of solemn-faced women and staring children in remote corners of the county.

Joe Meuse got the news about nine in the morning, from Sam Francis, who had been waiting in the village for the stores to open to get a plug of tobacco. Joe Meuse stepped over to John Paul's cabin to tell his friend. John was not to be seen in his usual place under the maple tree, and when he pushed open the door of John's cabin, he discovered Mary sitting idle and listless beside the unlighted stove. Joe Meuse stared.

"Where John Paul?"

"Gone."

"Where?"

"Don't know, said give you this," and she handed him the chipped pyramid of sandstone.

Joe Meuse took the stone in his hand, hefted it, smelt of it and stared at it in amazement; whatever did John Paul mean!

Then his quick eyes roaming about the room, fell on a blotch of dull crimson on the boards of the floor, and a second later upon a piece of splintered studding. He stepped quickly to the wall; a bullet was sticking in the beam. He took out his jackknife, skillfully cut an oblong piece from the studding, extracted the bullet, put it deep in his trousers pocket and plugged the hole. An examination of his friend's deep tracks to the river bank, linked to the news of the missing man and his own suspicions, revealed to him the whole story.

18

"Here you," he said to Mary after his swift return to the cabin, "get sand and scrub floor. Make him white like always; then weave baskets. I go step in John Paul's tracks and drag spruce from cabin to river."

In a little while everything was as Joe Meuse wished it. Mary had scrubbed the floor clean and sat at the door making a basket; he had smoked the wooden patch he had made in the studding, scuffed up John Paul's dooryard, and washed out the path, by which Alan Freeman must have approached the cabin, with many buckets of water; the track to the river was hidden by the heavy spruce he had dragged to and fro and eventually thrown in the river. He hoped the whites would not use dogs, but even if they did the scent would be light, for he had heard gusty showers rattle on his roof throughout the night.

It was late afternoon before a posse of searching white men headed by Lawyer Freeman and Sheriff Hardwick came up the river road. Alan Freeman, it was rumoured, had last been seen headed in that direction. Joe Meuse, in answer to Lawyer Freeman's queries as to the whereabouts of John Paul—the old man had counted upon John as his most skilful searcher—replied that his friend had gone far beyond Lac Joli towards the Tusket waters in search of ash wood and might not return for many days. Then with other Indians, he joined the searchers and made many ingenious suggestions.

For a week the searchers combed the nearby woods, halloing, blowing horns, ringing bells, building great fires by night; they dragged all the neighbouring lakes, rivers, still-waters; they employed hounds—all to no avail. One by one the weaker fell off from the search and returned to their work or their idleness; Lawyer Freeman cursed the weaklings and tirelessly ranged the forest to direct operations. His wife, overcome with grief, had taken to her bed. David and Joe Meuse kept close to the old man. Once Joe was thoroughly alarmed; a troop of boy scouts found a fresh-cut but muddied spruce on the shore at the foot of the long rapid. The white men examined it, but it told them nothing. Joe feared the children, whose minds had not been dulled with schooling; they were less foolish, he thought, than their fathers. That night, fearful lest the scouts might find the fresh-cut stump, close to John's cabin, he sawed the stump off flush with the ground and covered the sawn end with moss and black mud. All day he had been fearful lest the prying children might find the stump; now his mind was at ease, for the muddied spruce might have been cut twenty miles up river, for all the whites might know.

It was only at the end of ten days that Lawyer Freeman noted that John Paul was still absent, and began to suspect some connection between the absence of the Indian and the mysterious disappearance of his son. One of John's canoes lay on the river bank near tidewater, where he had left it on his return from Spar Lake with the sick hunter, but his other canoe, which Lawyer Freeman knew he kept on the upper still-water, was missing. Mary and Joe Meuse were questioned sharply, but they stuck to their original story; they had neither seen nor heard anything of Alan Freeman; John Paul had returned from his hunting trip, slept the night in his cabin, and set out early next morning in search of ash wood. He had taken rifle, shot-gun, and dunnage bags with him. There would be no more hunting parties to guide that season; perhaps John had gone to visit friends and relatives on the Shelburne or Tusket waters; sometimes he was away for weeks on end. The old man searched John Paul's cabin, poked into every hole and corner and found nothing.

At last the indomitable old man himself gave up the hopeless quest and walked daily to his office, shoulders bent and eyes upon the ground. He was stricken with sorrow but not beaten. He had always feared that the wild and wayward Alan, his first born, would come to some violent or disastrous end. He seldom spoke of his lost boy, but the mystery of his disappearance haunted him day and night like a phantom, and added greatly to his sorrow. He became convinced that if John Paul were living, he must know the secret. Somehow by hook or crook he must find John Paul.

One day when Mary was selling baskets in the village street, he leaned from his office window and called for her to come up.

"Mary, what did Alan say when he first came to your cabin that night?" he asked cunningly.

"He no come, me no see your son," was the sullen reply.

"Has John Paul come home?"

"No."

"Where is he?"

"Me no know. Hunt some place. Gone for ash wood. Tusket River maybe. Come back when ready."

"All right," he said, pulling out a roll of greenbacks, "you know where he is but you won't tell."

"Me no know where John Paul is."

"There's a hundred dollars for you any day you want to tell me. Understand?"

"Me no know where John Paul is."

"You know. Remember the hundred dollars is always waiting for you."

Mary went out mutely, and Lawyer Freeman buried his hands in his white hair, set his jaw and again racked his brain for some clue to the solution of the haunting mystery.

John Paul had calculated well, for no trace of Alan Freeman's body was ever found. The rapid had battered the poor limp thing against jagged rocks, the first ebb had borne it far out into the Basin, past nets and fish seines, which it seemed to clutch at with wavering hands; the next flood had washed it back against the leader of a mackerel trap, the following ebb swirled it swiftly through Digby Gut, to be lost forever to the sight of men in the red tides of Fundy Bay.

To the villagers the disappearance of Indian and wastrel white soon became only a topic of conversation; something interesting that had happened to break the dull monotony of their uninteresting lives. Young Freeman's demise they reckoned was a good riddance, but John Paul was a real loss to the community. Where could such another guide be found! No one could make axe and pick handles like John Paul. Louis Toney and Noel Malti, too lazy to search far afield for ash wood, made theirs of fir, that looked like ash but splintered at the first hard blow. If John Paul had done away with Freeman, they reasoned, it had been Freeman's fault. John Paul had always been a quiet unoffending Indian.

Perhaps Alan Freeman had killed John Paul and fled to the States, where an odd murderer or two made no difierence. Some hinted at Mary as a source of quarrel, but none but Mary and Joe Meuse, inscrutable and silent ones, knew. The mystery attracted and teased them; besides it was a story with a middle but with no beginning or end; only a morsel sweet to retail to gaping strangers as they sat of chilly evenings on nail kegs around the stove of the village store, looked knowing, told their special versions and opinions, and spat tobacco juice with unerring aim into the sawdust box, provided for their convenience and the storekeeper's protection.

Not so with Joe Meuse! He had hidden the chipped pyramid of sandstone under the root of a big rock maple near his cabin. Every day when he was surely alone, he used to steal down and examine the stone, turning it over and fingering it with care.

What did John Paul mean? What was the object behind the symbol? It was a definite message, that he knew, if he could but read it. During the two weeks that he had followed Lawyer Freeman through the woods on a useless quest, and sought with pretended eagerness for the body of Alan Freeman, he had thought of nothing but the meaning of the chipped sandstone. He was completely baffled.

One evening after the search was long spent, he slipped down to his maple tree, felt under the root and fished out the stone. He looked at it in despair and wrinkled his brow in hard thinking but no answer came to the problem. He lifted it in both hands as he had often done before, to search for some mark or inscription on its bottom, and in the vague light of early evening got it silhouetted against a patch of sky. In a flash he saw the Great Rock, the grey pyramid on Big Lake that he and John Paul had twice climbed. He threw down the stone, and danced with joy. Now he knew what the chipped sandstone meant. Good, John Paul was there and in safety; no one would seek him so far away. How blind he had been; why had he not guessed before? He had been as stupid as a white man. None but himself, not even Mary knew the secret hiding place. He would go to John Paul, but not for a long time, for John Paul's friend would be watched. It would take a week to go to the Great Rock and return and he must have a good excuse for such a long absence. Already there were night flurries of November snow, and he dared leave no tracks on such a journey. John Paul must wait for him till spring.

The Watchtower

The sun crept around the shoulder of the Rock, and at last touched John Paul's face. He awoke with a start, sat up, and looked wildly about him, then smiling, lay back in the nest he had formed, and let the long grasses slip through his fingers. Though back and shoulder blades still ached, safety and rest were sweet after a day and night of weariness and black terror. Never through that night of paddling and portaging had he been able to shake off the dark figure that had perched astride the sternpost of his canoe, and followed close at his heels on the carries. Now the morning sunlight had chased it away, and for a little while he lay inert, enjoying his freedom and safety.

Then he sprang up, stretched arms and legs, clambered to the top of the great Rock, and looked up and down the lake; there was not a speck upon its gleaming surface. The crisp morning breeze struck upon his face and ruffled his hair; his eyes ranged gladly over the vast panorama of lake, forest, bog and still-water, and he shouted in joy and defiance. Here no White Man's Law reigned; here was the law of tree, bird and wild thing. He was free! He would miss Mary and Joe Meuse; he regretted what his former friends Lawyer Freeman and young David would think of him, for they would never know the facts; but on the whole he was glad that he had escaped civilization and wondered, as he stood there on the Rock's summit, how he had endured it so long. Here he would live; here he would die.

Hunger assailed him, gnawing at his entrails; he had eaten nothing in two days. But there were things to be done before he could eat in safety. He leaped down from the rock, ran down the slope to his canoe in the yellow reeds, unloaded her, and carried her to a secure hiding place, among thick young spruces. He took his tumpline, and backed all his possessions to the southern base of the rock, where he found for them a temporary shelter from wind and weather in dry horizontal clefts. This done, he pulled up some fern roots, ate them with pieces of bread and raw bacon and drank deep draughts from the brook. He could build no fire till night fell, and then only a tiny one in some deep hollow, for the flare of fire touched the sky, and smoke scent carried a long way to the nose of an Indian. He was weary; he lay down and slept again in the autumn sunshine.

The next day, he began his preparations for a lifetime on the

Rock. These preparations lasted over many days. First he explored the Rock itself thoroughly and looked into every cleft. It was of grey granite, lichen-covered, colossal; such a stone, he reckoned Glooscap might have flung after his enemy, the fleeing beaver, though his favourite missile had been an island. The southern side of the Rock, nearest the forest, was sloping and easy of access, as shelves and notches served as steps; the northern side, facing the lake, was precipitous. Near the base, on the eastern side, were many gaping clefts where frost had been at work. Around the Rock's base were clumps of sweet fern and thick untrodden brown-top. On the very summit, John Paul found the tub-like cavity some eight feet across that he remembered, and in the cavity five rounded stones. He knew, from his own observation, that these hard rounded stones twirled by rushing water had ground out the pot-hole in a soft part of the granite, but he was puzzled to imagine how rushing water had ever reached so high. He had no information on glacial rivers, and knew nothing of the Rock's journey from the north. Perhaps, he said, smiling to himself, in the time of the great flood the priest had told them of. A grand story that, about pairs of all the animals in the world shut up in a big boat floating about the seas. A story was a story, and a true thing a true thing; the whites thought the Indians children, but the whites themselves were children. How often had he and Joe Meuse, when alone, laughed at that story and talked of the troubles of Mister Noah in keeping the peace in such a turbulent family. Well, he could laugh at the story no more, for he could think of no way that the pot-hole could have been formed save by a great flood. That the Rock was immensely old and that it had been on the hillside since the beginning of things, John Paul knew. Its hoary age inspired in him awe and reverence; it must have acquired great wisdom by staring through ages at lake and forest. From the first, he felt that the Rock might become a friend, who could give sage advice and shelter him in time of trouble. The Rock watched the lake with stern intensity; here, too, he should watch and the pot-hole should be his home and watchtower. At first he thought that he should throw out the grinding stones and give himself more room, but they seemed so ancient that he could not bring himself to do it; instead, he piled them up into a little shrine. The bottom he lined thickly with armfuls of dried moss and sweet fern, and on it laid his sheep-skin; over all he rigged his square of canvas as a protection against wind and weather. The outside of the canvas he smeared with clay and powdered stone, till its colour blended with the great stone. His watchtower was for the time complete; here he would spend hours by day and night, smoking, thinking, watching, as the Rock watched, for a speck upon the lake; no one, he knew, could come at him from behind through the forest.

He repacked all his stores, counted his matches, tied bundles of twenty in envelopes of birchbark, and laid them in a deep dry cleft. He could strike fire with whirling sticks if necessity demanded, but it was a great bother. Mikumwess, the mischievous prying little men, dwelt in such clefts, he had heard, but were they real? Perhaps as real as Noah and his ark! However, he knew that they feared fire, and hence would not tamper with his matches. His bread, flour, bacon, and ammunition he enveloped in great rolls of birchbark, stuffed them in deep rifts, and closed the rifts with stones against the prying paw of a bear. This was but a temporary arrangement.

In succeeding days he explored the nearby woods, and in the heart of an almost impenetrable growth of young spruce and fir, built himself a lodge, the front of upright poles, after the manner of the early Micmacs. The crevices he stuffed with clay and moss, and shingled the roof with hemlock slabs, carrying these from far up the brook since he wished to have no trace of man's hand near his Rock. Within, he made a table and bench, and nailed shelves and wooden hooks about the walls. He built stove and chimney of fire clay and whin rock, that would neither splinter nor explode in heat.

To his lodge when completed and weather-proof, he carried his gun, fishing gear, ammunition and provisions, and hung them on hooks or laid them on the shelves built around the wall. The lodge would serve as a hiding place for all his gear, if any canoes came on the lake, though himself he would never trust to such a hiding place. In time of danger, if driven from the Rock, his place of safety would be the depth of the forest behind him. He always approached his lodge by some different and devious route so as to form no path. Chips and splinters which he had made in its construction, he picked up one by one, burned them in a deep hole, and cast the ashes into the brook.

During all the time of his work upon the lodge, there was no half hour of day or night, when he was not on his watchtower, peering east, peering north across the bogs, peering longest and most carefully towards the west, his own way of approach, which Indians and a few whites might know. In fact, though he often tried to sit or sleep within his lodge, whither he would be sometimes driven by wind-blown rain, he had there no ease of heart. After a short stay in the warmth of his shelter, he would begin to be shaken and uncertain, and back he would go to his watchtower. A strange confidence in the Rock as his friend grew and grew; the Rock and the loons upon the lake were his sentries. He remembered the story his grandfather had told him: how Glooscap had at first taken Kwemoo, the loon, for his dog, but dismissed him as dog and retained him only as messenger, when he absented himself overmuch. Two wolves Glooscap had then taken as dogs, one white, one black, to serve him by day and night. John Paul loved the impudent loon with his mocking cry, and understood why Glooscap had first chosen him for watcher. No strange thing stirred on the lake, or parted the alders along the shore, without a warning cry of danger from the loon. All the beasts and birds knew the cry as well as John Paul.

Before the heavy snows of winter came, John Paul's arrangements were tolerably complete. In his smoked traps set cunningly along the brook margin, he had taken many muskrats and a few mink and otter. Their skins he pegged out on split wood and set them at the base of his Rock in the southern sun to cure. He shot a prying black bear, and a young bull moose that one early morning came blundering across the brook, snorting for a cow. The sun-cured pelts of moose and bear he sewed into a coat and warm sleeping bag for his watchtower, saving the long-haired shanks for larrigans. From the otter, mink, and rat skins he made cap and warm mittens. Some day, he decided, he would have a coat made in regular Micmac fashion from a caribou hide. He would not freeze or starve; he could get trout through the ice at any time, and snare grouse and rabbits; perhaps when his precious bread was gone, he could eke out his flour as sour-dough till spring. With the spring Joe Meuse would surely come.

He must, he decided, have one more moose; the crusted snows of a long winter would grind out more than two pairs of moose shanks. In getting his second moose, John Paul had a strange adventure. One early morning of December, John Paul reluctantly bade farewell to his Rock, adjuring it to watch in his absence, and set out for the forest, rifle slung over his shoulder. It was a perfect day for still-hunting; a fall of three inches of soft snow had been followed by a thaw that made the print of each footstep wet and slushy, and a restless gusty wind swept through the treetops. He followed the valley of the brook towards the southerly wooded hills, and in an alder cover, where a tributary brooklet made in, he found the fresh spoor of a big moose.

He soon came to the spot where the moose had guzzled through the snow to drink the sweet brook water, and then had turned in his tracks for his breakfast of birch twigs on the hard-wood ridge. John Paul followed the trail swiftly, yet with caution, stooping often to peer under low bows or through parted underbrush. Tracking conditions were perfect, for the whining southeast wind made such an uproar in the treetops, that it mattered not if twigs snapped beneath his feet. Halfway up the ridge the belt of spruces stopped abruptly; now he could see and be seen further through the leafless hardwoods. The spoor became fresher and fresher, with a tiny sparkle of water in the deep toe prints; here the moose had stopped to crop from a young birch. John Paul left the trail and made a deep half circle to leeward, so that the wind would blow from moose to him. He came in the direction of the trail again, creeping softly from cover to cover. Suddenly he spied an unusual swaying of a second-growth birch; then the great moose, unconscious of John Paul's presence, stepped into full view. He was a mighty one, with a great spread of many-notched antlers, slim-flanked, and deep shouldered, with low hanging dewlap. The background of snow made his sleek hide shine black as coal. With majestic dignity, his great head wove to and fro, snipping off the choicest buds of a yellow birch. Three cows were with him in the yard he had established; he was a worthy sultan of the ridge.

It was an easy shot, barely a hundred yards, but John Paul was so amused at the pride and self-satisfaction of that forest king, that for some ten minutes, he withheld his fire and crouched low to watch the movements of the bull. Something in common he had with the moose; here was a wild thing like himself disdainful of civilization and white men. Often before he had marvelled at the courage of the moose, who loped boldly across the open bog, lured by the seductive call of the birch horn to the very rifles of the hunters. He risked all for love; and even when sighting the hunter, stood disdainful and fearless, shaking his horns. John watched the moose enjoying his breakfast, till mindful of his own necessity for food, clothing, and dry warm shanks, he almost regretfully raised his rifle and fired. At the very instant when John Paul squeezed the trigger, the bull made a sudden and unexpected turn. The bullet did not find lodgment, as John had intended, behind the shoulder, but struck the great brute a slanting blow through the entrails, and pierced him through and through. With a snort of surprise, the bull made off along the ridge, followed by his three cows, crashing the trees as they ran. John hurried forward; the bull was bleeding from both sides; he had paunched him; a paunched moose will run far. Never had he missed so easy a shot; he was glad no whites were with him. Nothing left now but to follow the bull till he flagged through weariness, or dropped through exhaustion or loss of blood.

Along the ridge he went, noting tracks and twigs smeared with blood. Eastward the moose swerved down the ridge towards a bog dotted with clumps of hackmatacks. John followed to the margin and looked anxiously across the wide expanse. "Tugwegan," he muttered to himself in Micmac, meaning a place beyond some expanse which those who are crossing make for, without knowing whether they shall succeed. He ventured out upon the bog, it was hard going, the moose had sunk fetlock deep. The Rock, his crime, his watchfulness, his sense of imminent danger, were forgot in the instinct of the hunter. He was again a wild Micmac following the wounded moose, as many generations had done before him. The blurred sun stood at a dull zenith, still he plodded across the endless bog; the southeast wind hauled to a bitter draft out of the north, still he followed the moose; snow drifted in tiny flakes out of a leaden sky, dulling the edges of the deep tracks, still he followed the moose. At last he had crossed the great bog, but the moose had again swerved to the right towards the wooded hills near the head of his brook. He could tell by the dimmed tracks, that the cows had abandoned their slower, wounded master. Once on the top of a snowy ridge, his eyes caught a glimpse of a moving black spot, a bare half mile before him, and joy surged up in his hunter's heart.

As he loped along, he recalled the story of how Glooscap had first made the moose mountain large, higher than a lofty pine tree, and how when Glooscap had asked the moose: "What will you do to the men I shall create by shooting my arrows into the bark of ash trees?" The moose had replied: "I will crash the trees of the forest upon them." Then Glooscap had made the moose smaller and asked him: "Now what will you do?" And the moose had replied: "Now I will flee before man." Perhaps, he thought, Glooscap had forgotten to reduce this moose sufficiently, and he might flee before him for ever.

The snow fell faster and driven by the north wind snarled around the spruces; still John Paul held on. On a wooded knoll, near the headwaters of his brook and some twelve miles from his Rock, John Paul came up with the wounded monster. He was lying in the encrimsoned snow, his forelegs bent under him. Still he kept his head erect, his eyes glared defiance, his waving horns challenged to battle. As John approached, the moose struggled to his feet with one last effort, and staggered forward to meet his enemy. John put a bullet through his shoulder that crashed him down, and bled him on the spot.

Evening was coming, nearby he could hear the rush of the swollen brook that curved out behind his Rock, the snow was already a foot deep; he must camp in the open. It had turned bitter cold. With swift knife, he ripped the hide from the moose and let out blood and entrails. Next he felled six thick spruces and piled them up, interlacing their branches as a wind-break against the piercing gale from the north. To the southward of his wind-break, he dug out a circle in the snow, tramped the bottom hard, and covered it with a thick matting of spruce boughs. Then he set about getting firewood; a white birch cut into six foot lengths he piled on the south side of a circle for back logs, a dried spruce stub made his kindlings and small stuff. His open-top camp was complete. Darkness came quickly with intense frost; he stuffed rolls of birchbark beneath the dried spruce and applied a match. Up sprang a merry tongue of flame. John squatted before the fire and grilled moose steaks on sharpened forked sticks. He was hungry after the long tramp; the bull was an old one, but the steaks were tender and juicy. After he had eaten his fill, he got out his pipe and stuffed it with his tobacco, which he had eked out by mixing with the dried bark of red alder. His crime, his danger, his watch-tower on the Rock were for the time forgotten; he was happier than he had been for many a day. He puffed out great smoke clouds and, sitting on his heels before the blaze, he recalled the merry story of how Glooscap had taught the whale to smoke.

The whale had been a great friend to Glooscap, just as Qwahbeet the Beaver had always been his enemy. Once a sorcerer Winpe had stolen Glooscap's grandmother and Martin his younger brother, and left Glooscap imprisoned on an island. Then a friendly whale had hove in sight, and said: "Come, ride on my back." Glooscap had stepped on his back, but his weight was so great that the whale sank to the bottom of the sea. Glooscap cried, "Ho, you are too small, go fetch your uncle or your grandfather." Then the whale fetched his grandfather and Glooscap stepped on his back and floated. "Swim for the shore, grandfather," he cried, "I must overtake Winpe and get back Martin and my grandmother." The whale swam towards the mainland but he was afraid to go close in, lest he should ground, but Glooscap did not wish to wet his feet in the sea. The whale called to Glooscap: "How far are we from the coast?" Now they were quite close but crafty Glooscap, who did not want to soak his new larrigans in salt water, called back: "The shore looks like a bow-string of girl's hair." Then the whale went closer, till the clams, who were unfriendly to Glooscap, the big ones chanting in bass, the little ones in squeaky falsetto, warned grandfather whale that he was in shallow water. Then Glooscap leaped ashore dry-shod with a merry shout, and the whale cried: "I am ashore and undone." But Glooscap pushed him off with the point of his bow and headed him for deep water. Then the whale said: "I want my pay, I want a smoke." So Glooscap filled his pipe, lit it, and stuck it in the whale's jaw, who went off smoking and content. But Glooscap stood on the shore laughing at the whale smoking, and his merry laughter was heard from Cape Split to Passamaquoddy.

John Paul took his pipe from his mouth and grinned as he finished telling himself this old-time story. It had grown bitter cold; his front was warm from the glow of the great bed of embers, but his hinder parts were cold, as the outer air was sucked in behind him by the draft of the fire. His eye fell upon the moose hide; he picked it up and enveloped himself in it, green and bloody as it was. He wrapped the wide skin of the hind legs about his feet, the skin of the fore legs about his arms, dewlap and neck skin made a hood for his head. John Paul remembered that in Glooscap's time men could turn themselves into animals and back again at will. Now he was a moose-man. As he squatted before the blaze, he was deliciously warm front and rear and he began to doze fitfully. A strange picture he made in the cold silence of the wood broken only by the gusty wind, the crackle of the birch logs, and the rush of the brook. The fire blazed a circle of light in the enveloping darkness, glinted on the trunks of white birch, touched the encrimsoned snow, the heap of entrails and quarters of red meat, and made a high spot of John's dozing figure wrapped in the raw moose hide. Civilization was far off and forgotten.

With the break of day, John Paul left his open-top camp, and tramped twelve long woods miles through a foot and a half of snow back to his Rock. With much labour he poled his canoe up the flooded brook, loaded her with meat and hide, made a swift run downstream, and was back at the Rock for a second time by nightfall.

As he sat in his watchtower that night wrapped in furs, wearied but warm, he wondered, not only at his rashness in leaving the Rock for two days and a night in the season of still hunting, but also at some change that had taken place within him. For it was not quite the same John Paul who had come back to the Rock, to whom he recited his mighty hunting adventure in epic style; the night in the frozen snow-clad wood, wrapped in the green moose-hide, had awakened strange memories, whiffs from a far-off past, legend and fancy that he knew not when and how he had acquired.

The Strong Cold

VII THE STRONG COLD

John Paul's first winter on the Rock was his longest and hardest, for he was not yet inured to loneliness. In December the strong cold and big snows came; lake and still-water were frozen thick and snowed under; only the fiercest white-waters kept themselves unshackled. From his watchtower, lake and bog were now a flat expanse of dazzling white, manoeuvre room for an army corps. Behind him the hills were giant's furrows of snow, fringed along the horizon with bare gaunt hardwoods. In the lowlands, every bough of spruce, fir, and hemlock drooped beneath white burdens that cast blue shadows on the snow beneath. Not a bird twittered, the rabbit and Pulowech the partridge had burrowed deep, Kwemoo the loon, his watchful vidette, had flown southward; no sound now in that land of awful silence but the rumble of the white-water, which had changed its summer treble to a winter bass, the sharp crack of frost-struck granite, the sudden rending scream of the lake ice like the cry of a woman in pain. All of summer's kindliness was gone, all of fickle nature was now unfriendly to John Paul's soul and body.

For this reason he drew closer and closer to the Rock, that stood unchanged, immovable and indifferent to paltry change of time like the seasons. He loved its stolid indifference and indomitable pride. These were virtues his fathers had lauded. It had an ancient spirit, he knew, wisdom and secrets gleaned through the ages, which it would never yield to torture. As he lay in his nested hollow, wrapped in his moose-hide, otter cap drawn deep over ears and neck, his watchful eyes roaming the lake, he often drew off his clumsy mitten to pat the worn smooth surface beside him.

Short winter days were not so bad, for he busied himself with the duties of keeping alive, getting wood, making charcoal, oiling rifle, gun, and gear, spearing a fish, mending shanks and fur clothing. Even the worry of tracks made in the snow on his many visits to his spruce-hid lodge afforded some distraction, for he must set his mind upon obviating such marks of danger. Rough snowshoes he made— though he called them racquets—of ash wood and thongs of moose-hide, and with these he could glide over the crusted surface and leave little track behind him. When his eyes tired from watching the dazzling whiteness of the lake, and he lived in dread of snow blindness, he made himself a pair of rude glasses with wooden bows, the lenses of thin sheets of smoked mica that glistened everywhere in the brook rocks. John had seen white men, and Indians as well, blind as new born kittens from staring at the snow. His fear of snow blindness was great but he was almost glad of the fear, since two whole days were taken up with making the spectacles to obviate the danger.

But when early evening fell and black night followed, and the silence deepened, and the hours dragged slowly and nothing happened, then loneliness gnawed at his spirit. He had no light; he had no books and knew nothing of them; and he could not work with his hands in the darkness. Sometimes by night, as he dozed fitfully beside a spark of charcoal fire among the heaped-up grinding stones which served both as shrine and fireplace, strange fancies came upon him; the lake was peopled with human forms that lurked along the margins or raced with a cloud's shadow over the glistening surface. Waking suddenly, he would see them scattering for cover, and he would grasp his well-oiled rifle, feel for the extra clip of cartridges that lay on the rock shelf, and mutter: "Let them come on; they will be fewer before they reach the Rock top." Hordes of pursuers came, when ragged black clouds blew across the stars; he rejoiced in frosty, clear nights, when the full moon rode the sky, for then the lake was almost rid of his enemies.

Had it not been for the Rock, he might have gone mad, in the first long winter nights. His confidence in it as an understanding friend and protector grew steadily; to it, to while away the time, he told all his stories, legends, and secrets, his simple philosophy of life and nature; with it he reviewed the incidents of his crime, and the right and wrong of his action. He knew now, he told the Rock, though it had escaped interpretation at the time, why he had seen a sportive buck and doe on the forest shore of Lake Mulgrave on the day of his ill-fated home arrival. That was ever a sign of evil in the wigwam according to the old Micmac portents, outgrowth of his father's wisdom. He talked much of his crime; a white man would have done the same to him, had the positions been reversed. He had heard of one white man killing another in such a situation and going scot-free. Would he have killed a fellow Indian, if he had caught him with Mary? No, though he would have beaten and bruised him. The Indian tradition was different; the old Micmacs had been generous with their wives to noble strangers. Women were women, whom Glooscap had made to serve the braves and keep their wigwams. They were weak, the property of the conqueror, and must serve their needs. But for a white man to sneak into an Indian's cabin and take his squaw, that was another matter. The priest and the white man's God told him that was evil. The insolent white deserved death for taking the Indian's woman, when he had many white girls of his own. He was glad he had killed Alan Freeman, but he felt no grudge nor resentment against Mary. He wanted her; perhaps Joe Meuse would bring her, when he came in the spring. He could not blame her; it had been the white man's fault, and his heart leapt with gladness at the thought of the huddled white upon the floor. For once his race had asserted itself. How sweet it had been to lift the limp body, swing it upon his shoulder, and lug it to the rapid. Yes, Mary might come with Joe Meuse in the spring; he needed her, he yearned for her, loneliness was more terrible than cold or short rations. Yet he whispered to the Rock that he knew she would not come.

One dark moonless night, John Paul's Rock shuddered with the slight tremor of an earthquake. He was unafraid but sorry for his great friend, and laid his arm protectingly upon its shoulder. Kuhkw the rogue, the earthquake maker, whom Glooscap had but partly conquered, was at work in the bowels of the earth. How great were the forces of Nature that made even his great Rock shudder, as a canoe trembles in the crazy waves at the foot of a whitewater. Perhaps his Rock, and the mountains, and all the land floated in the sea or in something deeper than the sea. Some rock was made by fire, he knew, some laid down by water. There was the hard beautiful flint, from which his fathers had chipped arrows, darts, and fishing spears. Anyone could see that flint had been boiled up in some terrific heat. White hunters had told him of volcanoes and lava; perhaps the mountains and the land floated in a sea of melted rock. At the shudder of the Rock, John Paul remembered that long ago when many Indians were gathered far in the north to allot hunting territories to the tribes and families, there had once come a frightful commotion, a heaving and rumbling of the ground, and they were sore afraid. Then Glooscap had stood before them and said: "I go away now, but I shall return again; when you feel the rocks tremble, then know it is I. So then you will know when the last great war is to be, for then I shall make the ground shake with an awful noise." The priest had told him the story of how God had made the white man's world and all things therein, but it seemed to him no finer or truer than the old Micmac story.

Muntu the great Being, the divine one, had made the world, or at any rate if he had not made it, he had been with it from the beginning. But Glooscap had made man and all the trees, plants and rocks useful to man. He and Malsumsis had been twins, but while Glooscap was born in the natural way, Malsumsis sprang through his mother's side beneath the arm-pit, and killed her at his birth. Mischief and wickedness began at his birth, grew as he grew, and so baneful to man did he become that at last Glooscap killed his twin brother with the blow of a fern-root, the only thing in the world with which Malsumsis could be injured. Glooscap had come into the land of the Wabanaki out of the sunrise, in a great granite canoe covered with trees. The animals he had brought with him, and man he had shaped afterwards. First he made the Mikumwess, the elves, little men, dwellers in rocks; then he made man by taking his bow and shooting arrows into the ash-tree. As the arrows struck the ash-tree the Indians sprang from the bark, and hence the Mikumwess called them tree-men. Glooscap, maker and lover of men, saw that men were the noblest and greatest of all things created and he decided to protect them against the animals. First he called to him Team the moose, gigantic in size, and said to him: "What would you do if you saw an Indian coming?"

And the moose replied: "I should crash down the trees on him." Then Glooscap reduced him to his present shape and asked: "What should you do now?" And the moose looking down shamefaced replied: "I should run through the woods before him." Next Glooscap turned to the squirrel, that in those days was very fierce and larger than a wolf, and said: "What would you do if you met an Indian?" And the squirrel answered: "I should scratch the trees down on him." Then Glooscap took the squirrel in his hands and smoothed him down, till he grew smaller and smaller, as he is today. But the squirrel was for a long time Glooscap's dog, and he could grow large and fierce again at Glooscap's will and destroy the most terrible enemies. Now when Glooscap asked the great white bear what he should do if he met an Indian, the great bear replied succinctly: "Eat him." Whereupon Glooscap commanded him to go and live among rocks and ice, where he would see no Indians. And for a time Glooscap took Kwemoo the loon for his dog, but he was too great a wanderer, and instead Glooscap took two wolves, one black and one white, but the loons always remained his tale bearers. With these old tales and legends that he had heard around camp-fires in a hundred forms since childhood, John entertained himself and his great friend as he watched through long nights.

When the moon shone clear he reflected on how good Glooscap had been to the Indians. At first, he told the Rock, it was so dark that they could not see their weapons clearly to slay their enemies. Glooscap had given men light. Glooscap had taught them how to hunt, to build weirs and canoes, and how to shape arrowheads, spears, and nets. He had shown them the hidden virtues of plants, roots, and barks, had revealed the mysteries of dyes, especially the blood root and alder bark, and yellow ochre, had pointed out the wild vegetables that might be used as food, as well as the kinds of animals, birds, and fish that might be eaten. He loved the men he had created, and though he dwelt in the wilderness, his spirit was never far from the Indians at any time. Whenever they sought him bravely, they could find him in a lonely land. All over the land of the Wabanaki, he has left his name; hills, rocks, rivers, lakes, and islands bore witness to him. Last of all he taught the Indians the names of the stars.

From his recumbent position on the Rock's top, John had more time to look at the stars and to meditate upon them than ever before. He saw Orion stride across the sky, his great Dog at his heels in pursuit of Taurus, the Bull. Glorious Capella followed stately Perseus and majestic Andromeda. The Great Bear and Polaris he had noted long since, and used as compass and timepiece. He did not call the stars by these names, nor knew he aught of the peoples who had given them these poetic appellations. He called the stars and the constellations by names Glooscap had given to his fathers. From boyhood he had learned to associate the rising of certain stars and constellations with the coming of spring, the heat of summer, the sullen hush of autumn, the dull unfriendly cold of winter, or with the time of dripping icicles, the coming of wild geese and bluewings, the first arbutus, fireweed on the hills, the glow of the goldenrod, the fall of the leaf, moose-calling time.

He watched the constellations swing across the sky and fade with the glimmer of dawn. Where did they go? Doubtless Glooscap lit them and put them out. Some of the stars were friendly, some cold and distant, some twinkled, some shone steady, some were golden yellow, some burned copper red. Glooscap and his helpers must be kept busy pulling them across the sky. Around camp-fires he had heard white men say that the stars were other worlds and suns. How could they know that? That was child's talk. It was better as the Micmacs thought; the stars were the souls of Indian braves, and when the shooting stars fell in autumn, those souls came back to earth to enter new bodies. Was not a child often like his grandfather, in face, form, and character? It was clear that the grandfather's soul had come back upon the earth. One thing sorely puzzled him: why had not Glooscap in his greatness of heart for man, made enough moons to light all the nights, and why did the moon wax and wane every month? A moon that did not fade would have been a boon to him in his lonely watches. Sometimes of a clear night, he saw a wandering star that had three tiny points of light dancing about it. Why were the stars so thick in the middle streak? He wondered what made the snows come, the cold of winter, the flowers and heat of summer. Who dug out the lakes and started the brooks; who planted his great Rock on the hillside? Had it sheltered a man before, or had Muntu placed it there for him alone?

Would that first winter never pass! Days were short, but nights of fitful slumber endless long. How he yearned for Joe Meuse and Mary! Would Joe bring Mary with him? In his inmost heart, he knew that she would not dare to come without his order. In March, his flour gave out; now he had nothing to eat but fish or the flesh of beast or bird. He sickened of these and ate only when he was deathly faint or his strength failed. He was as lean and spare as an arrow. He craved bread by day, and at night, in restless slumber, dreamed of brown crusty loaves, fresh from Mary's oven. This blight, civilization had cast upon him. Would the spring and Joe Meuse never come! Even when he talked of the stars, and ancient legends, the coming of spring and Joe Meuse was always in the back of his mind. Far down the dim lake he would see the black speck that would mean his canoe, and he would rush madly down the slope, and wait for him among the yellow reeds.

The Coming of Spring

One mid-afternoon of late March as John Paul lay in his watchtower, he heard an unaccustomed rhythmic tapping. Cautiously, he peeped over his Rock's edge to find the cause. The icicles on the southern side of his Rock were dripping. He uttered a whoop of joy. The sun was beginning to eat up ice and snow. Now spring was surely coming. Next day he hacked the maple trees, and beneath the gashes hung wooden pails he had made for that purpose. The sap ran merrily; John Paul could scarcely keep up with it; two and sometimes three buckets a day ran from the big trees. In lieu of a boiling down pan, John used his two big camp kettles, storing the sap in tubs till he could get room to boil it. Under the kettles he kept brisk fires burning. To and fro from fire to dripping trees, he trudged through the snow. He forgot all his troubles and felt himself almost happy in this visible and tangible promise of spring. It was slow work but John had both time and patience. In the end, he had a fine lot of syrup and maple sugar, enough, he thought, to last him for a whole year. The syrup he poured into rude buckets, the blocks of sugar he wrapped in birch bark and stored away upon the shelves of his lodge. On the margin of the brook, he dug beneath the melting snow, to find the roots of succulent ferns. These he ground into a paste, fried them in bacon fat, and ate these cakes after covering them with thick maple syrup. He stopped in the midst of eating his cakes, and laughed aloud, as he thought how soon Joe Meuse would come with bread. As a culmination to this banquet, and as a celebration of the arrival of spring, he smoked a pipe of clear tobacco that had no alder bark in it.

Gradually the lake ice changed on the margins from blue whites to yellow browns, as the long imprisoned water seeped up through the dead reeds. One day, far out on the lake there was a patch of blue that widened with the hours, and towards night a V of geese circled, hovered, swooped, and splashed for a rest on the long journey north. With hand-cupped ear, John on the Rock's top could hear the clack of their solemn gossip. An hour before dawn, he crawled out on the rotten ice and sniped two ganders; now that his bacon was almost gone, he needed their fat.

Patches of brown began to show along the slope from Rock to lake, and on the hummocks the arbutus pushed out its mat of olive green leaves, among which were clusters of pink, delicately perfumed flowers. The cold wind from the melting lake ice bore their sweet scent to John Paul on his watchtower, and made him toss his head like a colt that is loosed in the pasture. In the tops of the maples came a hint of magenta, the willows waved their hanging catkins, among the birches was a promise of yellow. Big puffy wind clouds, swollen with importance, came sailing out of the south to cross an infinite blue. The ice broke into cakes, which wind and wave churned to fragments. More geese came, going northward, and after them the black ducks. The swollen brook exulted in its freedom, and changed its tune to piping treble; in the pool at the foot of the rapid, the trout were taking the May-fly. Now it was time for Joe to come, and John Paul began to watch with a new motive.

Intruders

IX INTRUDERS

One April night, as John tired by watching and waiting and ill at ease through bread hunger, dozed in his tower, he had a terrible dream. He dreamt that a great monster had swallowed all the water in the world. His great lake was drained, his brook-bed dry. Trout, perch, and giant musquellunge flapped and panted feebly on the lake bottom, and died in the heat of the sun. His mouth was dry and parched as an autumn leaf, he had naught to drink, he was perishing of thirst. He went to the monster, who sat before a cliff of red sandstone at the brook's headwaters, where he had built himself a dam to supply his own greedy needs. John Paul implored him to give him and the animals water. For the animals had gone with John Paul,—the moose, the black bear, the squirrel, the eel, who alone of fish travels overland. The monster gave John Paul a spoonful of muddy water, and laughed the animals to scorn. "Let them die," he said. There he sat embracing his great yellow paunch, tight and hard as a drumhead, for he was full of all the water in the world. Then John Paul and the animals had a conference, and racked their brains in vain. At last the clever eel said: "If we could make him laugh he might burst. I'll try." So the eel stood up on the very tip of his tail, and danced before the monster, the monster blinked his scornful half-open eyes; the eel danced faster, the monster winked; the eel tied himself in a knot and danced on, the monster grinned; the eel sprang high into the air and landed on very tail tip, the monster laughed; the eel did fin springs and cartwheels, the monster yelled and groaned with laughter—holding both hands on his trembling paunch; the eel did his best turn, sticking his tail tip in his mouth he rolled around the monster like a hoop, the monster bellowed and roared; he put up one hand to wipe the tears from his eyes, his belly burst, the flood gushed out, sweeping John and the animals down the brook into the lake.

As the cold water overwhelmed him, John Paul awoke trembling and wet with sweat. Instinctively he reached out and placed his hand on the shoulder of his protector, then glanced up and down the lake. Nothing in sight in the cold light of dawn! Still that dream meant something, John Paul knew; dreams were not sent for naught through a man's head. He remembered as he had swirled down the brook in company with the black bear, he had caught a glimpse of the monster shrunk to nothing but a common frog. That was Malsumsis the bad spirit at his pranks; it was plain that evil should come to him somehow by water. The eel must have been Glooscap, always on the side of men and animals, who had employed powerful magic— m'teoulin, John muttered to himself—to overcome Malsumsis. The dream had promised evil and deliverance; he would be watchful.

That very afternoon his roving eye caught a speck upon the lake, and a flash by its side in the sunlight. It was a canoe! It was Joe Meuse coming at last. In his joy he forgot all about the warning dream. He leaped from his watchtower, and raced down the slope toward the reeds to peer out across the level lake. From there he could see nothing. He ran to and fro, he laughed, he shouted, he threw himself on the ground and rolled in the dead leaves and grasses. He hurried back to his watchtower so that he might see his friend and signal to him. How slow the canoe moved, it was where it had been before. An hour he waited eagerly, the lake was long and the wind headed the canoe. Now the canoe was nearer, and as she veered in a gusty squall, he saw paddles flashing bow and stern. His heart thumped with joy; there were two people in her; Joe had brought Mary with him. He thrilled with excitement, quivers of joy ran up and down his spine, his finger tips prickled. Never had the spring sun shone so gloriously, the brook made sweeter music, nor the willow branches moved so graciously in the breeze. Why did they paddle so slowly, had he been in the canoe he should have made it leap through every wave! The canoe came nearer, he could see both forms now. Telescoping his hands, he peered and peered to get certain sight of wife and friend. Again the canoe veered broadside in a squall and in a flash he saw that they were both men, and that they did not paddle Indian fashion. In an instant his wild joy was transposed into black terror. They were whites; they were headed straight for his Rock; above his head he saw a black arm as a clutching shadow, Law was upon him. For a moment, he stood frozen with fear, motionless as a part of his Rock; then he sprang to action. Hastily he dismantled his watchtower,—he had plenty of time, they could not land for half an hour—scattered his bed of dried leaves and ferns, and wrapping everything he kept at his Rock in his square of canvas, carried all to his lodge by a well-chosen line of retreat quite hidden from the lake. This done, he returned to the Rock, and with skill acquired in breaking many a camp, he restored everything as it was on his first arrival. No white man, he was sure, could detect that he had ever been there; now that the snows were gone, except in the shadow of the spruces, there were no paths or tracks to worry about. He crept close to the shoulder of the Rock, and peeped out cautiously. He had decided to abandon the Rock as a fortress, and retreat to the forest, where if they followed, he would still-hunt them, and kill both separately. That night he would loose their canoe, bottom up upon the lake. They were close now, yes, both whites, both bearded. He unslung his rifle, and for a moment was tempted to pick them off in their canoe, rather than to ambush or hunt them in the forest. No, the forest plan was surer; he might miss one, who could escape by keeping the canoe close under the high land.

He retreated to the forest, to the eastward of his Rock, and hid among thick young spruces, whence he could watch the intruders unseen. They ran their canoe into the reeds, hauled her out and unloaded her, collected wood, pitched a sagging tent, that made John Paul sniff scornfully, and while one built a fire and rummaged in the food-box, the other took his rod and began to whip the pool, where the brook made into the lake. When he had landed several trout, he returned to his fellow, and they sat down before the fire to fry their fish and to eat and drink. John Paul's lips watered, as one took a loaf of bread and cut off thick slices. John could not understand their actions; why had they not begun to search around the Rock? They were not Mooin River whites, he knew, but strangers, probably the sheriff and his deputy from Digby. John's eye followed their every move. By shifting a little to the right of his first position, he could get them in line and kill both with one shot. How stupid and insolently bold these whites were. He moved noiselessly, rested the muzzle of his rifle upon a branch, and took steady aim. It was a sure thing: he could get one through the head, one through the breast with a single shot. But John Paul was a sportsman, and this shot was so easy that he could not bring himself to press the trigger. As he waited, he hardly knew why, before destroying his pursuers, who he was convinced were trying to destroy him, he glanced through the branches at his great towering friend the Rock. And the Rock shouted to him in a voice of thunder: "Don't shoot, John Paul, wait!" John was astonished that the white men did not start up in terror at the sound of the mighty voice, but they remained calm and undisturbed. One was pouring himself a cup of coffee from a blackened camp kettle, the other stripped the backbone from the pink flesh of a trout. Obviously, he alone had heard; their deaf ears had not caught the sound of the Rock's voice.

John Paul heeded the injunction of the Rock and waited, squinting every little while along the sights of his rifle across the branch, as his fingers itched to press the trigger. Evening began to fall; the whites sat smoking and talking by their camp-fire; night settled down. Then John had a curious temptation: he was overcome by a desire to hear human voices, and to learn what they were talking about. Silent as a snake, he left the dark shadows of the spruces, and rifle in hand, wriggled on his belly towards the campfire. Soon he was near the whites, crouched in a hollow behind a hummock matted with the leaves of arbutus. He listened; he could hear every word they spoke. Soon he caught their drift and intention. He was glad he had not fired; the Rock had warned him truly. They made no mention of his name; they were not after him at all; they were prospectors seeking gold in the thick quartz vein at the eastern end of the lake. The sound of their voices was sweet to John's ears; he wanted to hate these white invaders and found that he could not. He crouched carelessly in the hollow now, hardly mastering an intense desire to step forward out of the darkness and sit with them at their camp-fire. So many comfortable nights he had sat around camp-fires, and they would doubtless proffer him bread and whiskey! Again he glanced toward his Rock for guidance, and its great head that towered to the stars visibly said, "No!" John realized that the Rock was right. It would be madness to reveal himself in his hiding place. How should he account for himself, what story would he tell, what tales might these prospectors not carry to Mooin River? Still the flow of voices was sweet, and to crunch the teeth through a crust of bread would be a heavenly pleasure.

Presently the whites threw a back-log upon their fire, and slipped into their sleeping bags within the tent. John listened till he heard deep breathing, then crept in close, lifted the tent flap and fumbled with groping hand in their provision box. He emerged with a loaf of bread, two figs of tobacco, a box of matches and a handful of cartridges. He had experience enough with careless whites to know that they would miss nothing, or even if they did, that they would blame it on a prowling bear, or find some cause without grounds. In the darkness, he held his pilfered treasure up to Muntu for a blessing. He would be blamed he knew by Jesus the carpenter's son, God of men in towns and cities, but Muntu, the hunter's God, understood an Indian's necessity. John watched till dawn, when the prospectors bestirred themselves, broke camp and were gone.

Joe Meuse

A month later John Paul, the watcher, saw another moving speck in the western end of the lake. It was early morning and the level rays of the sun just peeping over the hardwoods glinted on a wet paddle. Again John dismantled his watchtower, carried all to his lodge and crouched waiting in the hollow of his Rock. He would not be caught napping a second time. For hours he watched, motionless as a piece of his Rock. The canoe was near now. She was deeply laden and had but a single paddler, who swung his paddle Indian-fashion, and who every little while laid his paddle from gunwale to gunwale and stooped to pick up something that he held up in his hand against the sky. John Paul could not understand this strange movement, nor guess that Joe Meuse, for it was really he this time, had brought with him the symbol of chipped sandstone, and was holding it against the blue, to compare it with the shape of the great Rock.

It was a good imitation, Joe decided, and he had little doubt that John would be somewhere near the Rock, if his food had held out and if he had survived the cold of winter. He began to flash his paddle, in a peculiar way that he and John had used as boys. He and John had always been canoe mates, John in the stern, Joe in the bow. Only the summer before John Paul's flight, he and John had won the big canoe race at the carnival, darting beneath the Mooin River bridge two lengths ahead of their most dangerous rivals.

John Paul saw and recognized the paddle's twist, that made water fly and flash from stern to stem, yet he still crouched hidden in his watchtower. He must be sure this time; he had not forgotten the panic caused by his other mistake. The canoe came straight for him. He would wait on his friend the Rock; there was no need to retreat to the forest, for he could certainly deal with one man if he proved an enemy. The canoe entered the reeds, the man sprang out, drew his craft into safety, and advanced straight up the slope. It was an Indian; it was Joe Meuse beyond a shadow of a doubt. John Paul slung his rifle on his shoulder, leaped down from the sloping side of his Rock, and ran with great loping strides to meet the friend of his youth.

"Joe Meuse!"

"John Paul!"

They halted face to face, looked at one another in the restrained fashion of Indians, and for a little had nothing to say to one another.

John Paul's heart was so nigh to bursting with joy at the sight of his friend, that he dared not speak, for he knew a man should never wholly show what he feels intensely.

"Fetch grub," said Joe Meuse finally with a slow smile. "Come get him."

They walked down to the canoe, unloaded her and carried the stores to shelter. Joe Meuse had brought just the right things: socks, two pairs of stout khaki trousers and two shirts of like material, seed potatoes and seed corn and squash, four bags of flour, twelve big loaves of bread, a side of bacon, a two-bushel bag of salt, a box of fig tobacco, a big can of tea, a huge box of Mary's molasses cakes, cartridges, shells with powder and shot to load them, a mattock, a stout axe, a long shallow pan for boiling down sap, a package of flat files, fish hooks, a hank of fine strong gut, copper tacks, a can of white lead, and two bottles of whiskey. Joe had given a good deal of thought to the things John Paul would need.

"Got plenty sugar here, me no bring him," said Joe, nodding his head toward the maples.

"Yeh, plenty sugar here. How you pay for all, Joe?"

"Mary sell baskets. Me good luck with traps, buy different shops, different times."

Joe Meuse did not mention that he had slipped the four bags of flour off a truck that stood in front of Marshall's store, and under cover of darkness, dropped them into his nearby canoe.

"I come late, had to wait, had to hide grub in woods. Say I go hunt ash wood and fishin'. They watch maybe. Know me your friend."

"Find him?"

"No, eels got him."

"They know?"

"No, only guess."

"Why they think me run away?"

"Know nothin', only guess. Stupid white mans. Only old man Freeman, he ask Mary once where his boy, where you is. He think maybe."

"Ol' man Freeman he smart; he smart when I tak' him on hunt party."

"Yeh, he think maybe. How long stay here, John Paul?"

"All time. Me no want jail or hang."

"Hear white man say, no hang when can't find body. His body gone."

"Maybe white man no hang, Indian yes."

"Get to States bime-by maybe."

"No, no safe near white mens. Safe here in woods. Big Rock my friend."

"Winter cold?"

"Yeh, strong cold, but good trap along brook. Me got load back for you, ash sticks, maple sugar, birch oil, good otter, rat, mink, fox furs, one patch. You tak' 'em, sell slow an' bring grub nex' spring. Made plenty baskets too. You tak' 'em too."

"No tak' baskets, people know your shape and weave."

"Me weave 'em bad, lop-sided, ends stick out like Joe Toney's. Me weave 'em bad on purpose."

"No, me no tak' baskets. White mens no know, but Indians maybe."

The spring sunshine was glorious, Pulowech the partridge drummed in the wood, Kwemoo the loon rose from the depth of the lake to flap his wings, stretch his white-ringed neck and scream his saucy yell, trout splashed in the pool. John felt that Glooscap had sent this perfect day for his meeting with Joe. They sprawled in the dry grasses at the great Rock's base, and with the spring sunshine beating upon their shoulders, ate their lunch together. John treated himself to a great hunk of crusty bread Mary had baked. It was wonderful, it was heavenly, he drove his teeth savagely into the brown heel and kept the crumbs in his mouth a long time before swallowing them; nothing had ever tasted so sweet to him. Bacon sizzled in the pan; John Paul boldly took a chance on smoke that day. They topped off their banquet with two fat molasses cookies and stout pegs of whiskey. What joy for John Paul! After the meal, they smoked long pipes of tobacco, and lazily watched the smoke trail out in lines of brown and grey to waver and flicker around the shoulder of the rock. There was nothing much in the way of conversation, for there was nothing to say. Neither cared to waste words; they understood one another and everything essential had been communicated in the first few minutes of talk. John longed for some news of Mary but with a gentleman's instinct he asked no questions about her, nor even mentioned her name, nor did Joe Meuse volunteer any information. John looked at his friend and thought how fine it would be if Joe Meuse would stay with him always; daily they would eat and lounge thus in the grass far from insolent whites. That would be like the happy hunting ground. But no, that would be impossible; who then would bring him food?

Presently John broke silence: "Me left quick; you clean up maybe?"

"Yeh. Bring somethin' you lak have maybe."

Joe Meuse fumbled in his trousers' pocket and produced a twisted bullet.

"Yeh," said John Paul smiling and tucking it away carefully. "Me keep him, lucky bullet."

In mid-afternoon, Joe rose and stretched himself. "Me go now. Not good be away too long. Camp long portage tonight. Travel slow, three carries."

"Yeh," said John Paul without emotion. "Carry down load."

They placed the furs and woodland treasures in the canoe and Joe Meuse paddled off, stopping every now and then to look back, wave his paddle and flash it in their old-time way. From his watchtower, John Paul looked and looked, till the canoe dwindled to a speck, and faded into rocks, trees and evening mists. For another whole year he would be alone.

Forest Garden

The evening after Joe Meuse had departed was a melancholy time for John Paul. Joe was going back to the world of men to talk, to see women, to hear strange new things about the camp-fire; he was left alone, alone with his Rock at which for a little he looked with resentment. For a long time he sat brooding as evening began to fall, and the birds to call across the ravine from treetop to treetop; then rousing himself, he took the twisted bullet from his pocket, bored a hole through it and strung it upon a moose thong. He put his head through the loop of the thong, and let the bullet rest against his bare breast. There he would wear it to make him mindful, and watchful, and to bring him luck. For the saving of the bullet, that had meant so much to him, was in accord with the old Micmac idea that the head of spear or arrow that had killed some beast of the wood should never be used again, but preserved as a precious relic.

Next morning he set out on a new quest. Joe had brought him seeds and he must employ them for his self-support; he must find a garden plot well hidden and a goodly distance from his Rock. He walked along the ridge toward the south, looking down into the valley of the brook. Several times he stopped, made excursions into the valley and tried the ground, but each time returned dissatisfied, either with the shallowness and stoniness of the earth, or with the quality of the soil which he smelt, and rubbed between thumb and finger. At last, near the mouth of a tributary spring brook, he found the very patch he wanted, a plot of flat interval that met the hillside at an easy angle. John ground his heel into the soil; it was black leaf mould mingled with fine silt that the brook had washed down through the ages. He sharpened a stake and drove it down till he hit hard-pan; yes, two feet of good black soil and few stones. It would serve. A fringe of alders hid the roaring brook; halfway up the hillside were spruces, above them birches and maples. It was well hidden, yet the summer sun after it had climbed the eastern ridges would lie on it all day long.

With the mattock Joe had brought him, John began to skim off and pile the thick sod. It was no easy task, for there were some clumps of sweet fern and their roots went deep. Fortunately the stones were few, and there were no trees except a few shallow-rooted poplars. John made trenches about these, bent them down with his weight, snicked the tensed roots and tore them out with the strength of his hands. John grunted and often paused to wipe the sweat from his brow. It was hot work and around his head hovered a halo of no-see-'ems. Gardening was hateful to him by nature; it was really squaw's work, but now necessity drove him on.

He remembered having heard that Glooscap, departing for the far north after having taught the Indians the arts of basket-making and shaping flint implements, had last of all given them four rich gifts, the potato, the squash, Indian corn, the tobacco plant, and told the Indians how to plant and grow them. An idea from that story was born in his brain; he had the seed of squash, potato, corn. Why, since he was perforce a gardener, might he not grow tobacco plants on this hot sheltered hillside? Indian and habitant, he knew, raised coarse tobacco in the Province of Quebec; he would have Joe Meuse bring him tobacco plants, and raise his own supply of leaf. Then he need mix no alder bark with his tobacco, and through the livelong day he could puff smoke-clouds, as big as the clouds Glooskap's whale had raised.

John had no training in gardening, but he was intelligent and had observed how the whites set about it. He knew that new land needed no manure, that potatoes developed badly in too dry land, and rotted in wet land in a rainy season, that corn did well in dry land and needed much sunshine. His corn and two-thirds of his potatoes he planted on the hillside; the remainder of his potatoes he dropped in his furrowed interval. He gave plenty of room for his squash to spread— they were greedy runners— and set his beans shallow in straight rows wide apart. If a drought came, he could carry water from the brook to his hillside patch, but he could do little to drain his interval if floods came in a wet season. He would have planted on the hillside altogether, had not his flat interval been so temptingly rich and deep.

This labour of making his garden, tearing up sods, ferns and small trees, breaking and loosening the soil, preparing the furrows, cutting—each piece of potato must have an eye—dropping the seed and covering all with light firm dirt, took the greater part of two weeks, for he had no peace of mind did he not frequently return to his friend the Rock, to look up and down the lake's surface. As he scaled the southern slope he carried on some such conversation with the Rock, making answer and reply in different pitch and intonation.

"Anything on the lake, old watcher?"

"No speck as big as the point of a fish-spear."

"Keep good watch till I return."

"I see all that comes on the lake, though the streak be as fine as a bow-string of girl's hair."

"I plant a garden and ask a blessing of Glooscap."

"The Indian women of old planted squash and corn; I will watch as you work."

After days of repugnant and arduous labour in his garden plot, nights of early summer upon the Rock were sweet. The light lingered a long time, twilight fell gently. Sky and lake took changing colours; in the full light the sky was blue as a robin's egg, the lake grey-blue; greens and purples came with the twilight, and deepened into blues and black as the light faded. Birds called to one another from the treetops; far out on the lake, Kwemoo, the loon, hooted in derision of all save himself or sang his doleful but prophetic rain call; from some dead spruce stub Ko-ko-kas, the owl, called persistently to his mate across the ravine. John often thought of what the old Indians said at such times of loon and owl: "They are calling upon Glooscap." For loon and owl had been two of the hero's greatest friends. Yes, the summer season, after the strong cold of winter, was wonderful, perhaps Glooscap's greatest gift. A hundred times as he lay snug in his rock nest, puffing in great clouds his dried red alder bark mixed with a pinch of tobacco, and watching the lake, he told the Rock the story of how Glooscap had given the Indians summer.

N'karnayoo, in the old time, he always began this story to the Rock. Once, long ago, it was cold, for the Indians had only the pale light of sunrise or red twilight to warm and light them; otherwise it was dark. Then Glooscap set off and travelled north into the region of snow, ice and dreadful frost. There on a desolate ice field he found the wigwam of Winter. "Come in," called Winter gruffly, "come in and smoke." Then Glooscap entered and took the pipe proffered him, and he and Winter puffed big-bellied clouds at one another, swollen like those that sail across the summer sky. But neither could smoke the other out. It was powerful cold, the marrow within Glooscap's bones was chilled to ice, his teeth chattered loose. Then Winter used strong m'teoulin, magic, and froze Glooscap stiff as a board, and so Glooscap slept like a toad for six months. When he woke, Winter was dozing and he was free of his magic; he stole out softly, and hurried south. Warmer and warmer it grew, till he came to the land of the little people. Their beautiful young queen was Summer, and Glooscap stole her by a crafty trick, and carried her off in his bosom. The little people pursued him, but sly old Glooscap cut a moose hide into slender strips, tied the strips together, and let a long end trail from his pocket. The little men found the trailing end and stopped to pull Glooscap back by the thong, but Glooscap paid out line and thus escaped them. Back to the wigwam of Winter he carried the beautiful Queen Summer; there sat the old tyrant drowsing in a cake of ice. Glooscap touched him with the hand of Summer, and lo, Winter melted and ran in shining streams into the sea. Then Glooscap carried back Summer to the little people, and returned to the Indians, whom he loved. Now they dwelt no more in pale dawn and grey twilight, but in the full light of Summer days, for Winter was dead.

N'karnayoo, in the old times, he ended, smiling and looking at the Rock for approval, and thinking how grand it must have been to have lived in times past, when there were heroes upon the earth. The longer he was alone, the oftener he told the Rock these tales, heard as a child from the old men.

Yes, John Paul decided Glooscap's gift of summer to the Indians had been his greatest gift, for John's first summer on the Rock was a gracious season. In June came wild strawberries on the brook's hillsides, filling the air with their delicate perfume. John Paul's hands were stained red for many a day. After the strawberries, came thick clustering blueberries in burnt patches where lightning had done its work, and later the high-bush blueberries in swampy places about the lake. These he stripped off by handfuls. Then on stunted bushes among windfalls came the raspberries, that yield to the lightest touch of the picker's hand, and after them the blackberry bushes, on the edges of wooded places, bent beneath their burden of black fruit that glistened in the August sun. In late September wet places in the bogs gleamed red, so plentiful were the fox-berries and cranberries. John Paul wondered at the profusion and wastefulness of Nature; here was untouched fruit enough to feed people in many great cities. Beasts and birds of the forest ate of it, it was true, still there was abundance and to spare. He made small tubs of spruce wood, and after he had boiled down his berries with lumps of maple sugar, poured the rich conserve into these tubs, closed them with a round, close-fitting cover, and sealed the cracks with fine clay from the brook mouth. His blackberries he mashed in a large open tub, and set them in the sun to ferment. When after some weeks, he drew off the liquor with a siphon of moose-wood and mixed it with a little whiskey, it made a drink that put heart into a man. In fact, after John Paul's first inordinate trial, when he had tasted and tasted and smacked his lips over the rich liquor many times, he strode to the top of his Rock and made an oration, partly English, partly Micmac, with a little French patois interspersed, a eulogy of the greatness of Glooscap, and a general defiance of Law and the whole white race.

Summer passed gently into early autumn, and the swamp maples began to wave their banners of gold and crimson; it was time to think of garnering his garden stuff, and storing it against the long winter. In the new rich land his potatoes had grown tall and stalky, had flowered in late July, and now the tops were brown and wilted. John Paul had been cursed by neither blight nor potato bug, in his remote forest garden. In early September it was high time to dig them, though John knew that they kept better through the winter if left long in the ground. Already the grass in the bottom land had twice been white with early hoar frost. The corn that he had hilled up high against the wind had grown six and seven feet tall, the yellow tassels had come, had sifted their pollen on the breeze, and now the silk was brown and withered. John tested each ear between approving thumb and finger and slit open a few green sheaths, to mark with pleasure the firm yellow rows beneath. The pods of the low and pole beans were brown and full. But the squashes were the glory of John's garden. He had trained these to run up the hillside, where they would choke neither potatoes nor corn, for the squash is by nature an invader, a conqueror. Up the hill they had gone boldly, some to twine and cling about the stems of goldenrod; others meeting small spruces in their progress, scaled these, and now small yellow ovals that would not develop into full grown squashes swung pendant against the green spruce boughs. John had pinched off many of the little squashes on the ground, so that those left might develop, but he could not bring himself to pluck the pendant yellow ovals on spruce and goldenrod. In spite of his dislike of agriculture, John Paul, standing on the interval, waist-deep in meadow sweet and feathery wild parsnip, could not help but smile with pleasure at the riches of his garden, in the warm glow of an afternoon September sun.

One set of conditions produced another; now he must have a frostproof cellar. He tore up the floor of his lodge and with his mattock began to dig a hole and carry out the dirt by basketfuls. It was tedious and unpleasing work, but John, again driven by necessity, stuck to it and soon had an excavation six by eight feet across the top and nearly six feet deep. He made a floor of slate from a nearby fault and walled up the sides. It was hard work; every stone had to be carried a distance of at least a hundred feet. But at last it was laid and mortared with clay; straight and true the walls stood, though built with neither level nor plumb line.

Then John dug his potatoes, laid them in the hot sun to dry thoroughly, and towards evening bore them in baskets to his new-made cellar. Never did squirrel have more joy in hiding away his store of nuts against the cold of winter. The potatoes had grown well, five or six to the hill, large, well-formed and free from scab. He husked his corn, dried that too in the sun, and hung it in great festoons about the beams of his lodge. Beans he dried, shelled and stored in baskets. Last of all he gathered his fat yellow squashes, thirty-five of them in all, and laid them in the cellar by his potatoes. Now he would not starve nor suffer from meat diet alone; Glooscap had been gracious to him.

Later he improvised a hand mill, and when his corn was hard and dry, ground some into rough meal. This had been the food of the old Indians, and fried cakes of it began to taste sweeter to him than the white flour of civilization. No longer came that dreadful craving for crusted white bread, that had harassed him throughout his first winter.

The Lost Pipe

It was while John Paul was storing away his crops for the winter that he met with what seemed to him a serious disaster. One evening after a day of hard work, he climbed his Rock to rest, to watch, to smoke. Tobacco was a great comfort to John; he seldom smoked in the daytime, for he had to be saving, but often throughout the day he dreamed of his pipe at night, though the contents of the bowl might be two-thirds alder bark. Only on great occasions did he allow himself clear tobacco. On this particular evening, he lit a smudge on his Rock shrine to keep off the mosquitoes, and settling down in his soft snug nest, felt in his pocket for his pipe. It was not in its accustomed place. He fumbled through all his pockets, and patted his legs; no comforting lump revealed its presence. He sprang up in real dismay and searched in every crevice of his watchtower. It could not be found, it was gone, *he had lost his pipe.* He had brought but one with him, a time-honored friend, and Joe Meuse had not thought a second pipe essential to John's comfort. Down the Rock's face he scrambled, peering into every crack and crevice, and parting the grasses round its base. To his lodge he rushed wildly, and hunted everywhere; the pipe could not be found. Darkness was coming on; it was folly to search further. He returned to his watch-tower to go over in his mind every wooded spot, every open glade he had visited throughout the day. Perhaps it had hopped out of his pocket when he sprang over the windfall by the brook. He was restless without his pipe and spent a truly melancholy night; owl and loon mocked him. He thought of all the fine pipes he had smoked around camp-fires, of the whale with Glooscap's pipe in his jaw. There were hundreds of stories of Glooscap and tobacco, and try as he might he could not rid his mind of these.

N'karnayoo, in the old time, Glooscap had been a right valiant smoker. Once an evil-minded sorcerer had planned to murder Glooscap, and came to visit him in his lodge. Glooscap read his heart. The sorcerer proposed a competition in smoking, for in this he thought he could surpass Glooscap, and thus make him fearful, as one fish fears another that excels him in swimming. The sorcerer filled his pipe, lit it, and burning all the tomawe with one breath, blew a cloud of smoke through his nostrils. Then Glooscap took a pipe ten times larger than that of the sorcerer, filled, lit it, burned all the tomawe with one giant draw, and drove out through his nostrils smoke, flame, and cinders with such a roar that the ground opened in a chasm at his feet. Then the evil-minded sorcerer was frightened and ran away swiftly into the forest. A dozen such tales chased one another through John Paul's head, as throughout the night, restless and moody, he sat watching the lake and praying for dawn to come.

With the first light he was abroad, retracing every bit of woodland and brook bank he had visited the day before. He peered with keen eyes into every clump of grass and fern, with his fingers he raked the ground about the windfall he had jumped over, he ransacked rock and lodge, but the pipe could not be found. John Paul was angry, not only because of the discomfort occasioned by the loss of his pipe, but that he should lose anything. Losing was not a habit in his life. The garden was the only place left to search; he had hoed out a few potatoes on the previous day; perhaps the pipe had dropped unnoticed from his pocket and been covered with dirt. He took his mattock and carefully turned over the earth in his garden. The pipe could not be found. Another evening was coming; John Paul was in despair.

Then he remembered having heard that the old Indians sometimes used pitcher plants for pipes. He rushed off to a swamp, plucked a dozen of those strange carnivorous plants, washed flies and insects from them, and carried them off to his Rock. From the pitcher plant, with a great waste of tobacco and willow bark, he got a sad unsatisfactory smoke. Still it was something; he felt decidedly better and easier in his mind. Would it be necessary, he wondered, to visit some settlement to beg, buy or steal a pipe? Towards morning of this second night, he consulted his great friend the Rock and asked for a solution of his difficult problem.

"I have lost my pipe, lost my pipe like a white man. What shall I do, great friend?"

For a long time there was no reply; then in a deeper tone he answered for the Rock, by asking another question.

"Did not your fathers before you smoke?"

"They did."

"What did they smoke?"

"They smoked tomawe with willow and alder in great pipes of stone."

"Then make a great pipe of stone. Have the white men so spoiled you, that you have forgotten how to chip stone?"

In the silence of the night John Paul gave a whoop of joy; his great wise friend told him everything. Bright and early next morning he was searching the brook bottom for a piece of sandstone. This he soon found and chipped into the rough semblance of a pipe bowl. Then came the tedious work of hollowing out the bowl; this he accomplished skilfully with a file and the tip of a hard knife. Night fell before the bowl was hollowed, and of necessity he must again smoke his tobacco in pitcher plants. By noon the next day the bowl was ground out, and the slow painful process of boring a hole from the stem to the bowl began. This he achieved by sticking a short length of fox wire into a piece of alder wood, hardening the wire in the fire, filing the end to a cutting edge, and turning patiently. After a while he improved on his first process; he held the bowl between his knees, and having fixed a horizontal to hold the upper end of his alder stick, he twirled the upright between both hands, and made the wire spin in the stone. In three hours he was through. It was easy now to push the pith from a length of moose-wood, and letting it overlap the stem of stone, lash it firmly. He tried it in his lips; it drew without leaking where wood met stone. Hurrah, he had a capital pipe. He rushed back to his Rock, holding it out to his friend in triumph. He laughed, and filling his new pipe with clear tobacco, drove white clouds from his nostrils. Never had a pipe seemed so sweet, never smoking so satisfactory. In subsequent days he smoothed the outer surface of the bowl with a fine file, and polished it with dusty sand. With a sharp point of steel, he scratched an inscription about the bowl in the old Micmac sign language,

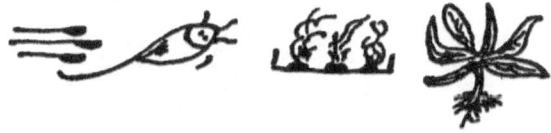

which means, Glooscap or Muntu burns tobacco. True, the priests had made the sign for Muntu stand for the devil, but John Paul knew better than that, for the true devil was Malsumsis or Lon, who was the enemy of Glooscap, Muntu and the Indians.

When he had more leisure, he made pipe stems of various lengths, some so long that he could recline at his ease, stretched out in his nest, and rest his pipe bowl on a little rock shelf to one side. From his long pipe stems of moose-wood he stripped the bark at intervals, and stained the bared wood with red from the alder root or yellow from coptis trifolia, golden thread. He was so pleased with these pipe stems that his interest in colour was reawakened. There were no Diamond Dyes in the forest, but the distilled juices of strawberry, blueberry, blackberry, cranberry, and the natural juices of alder and golden thread, made rich lasting stains upon white wood. He taught himself to form small vases of clay and harden them, and in these he stored his pigments. He took more delight in his great pipe with its gay coloured stems, than in anything he had made in all his life before. He resolved that he should never lose this pipe, because he would never take it from his watchtower; there awaiting him on the Rock shelf it should always remain.

The chill of autumn was upon him, the lake was deep blue at midday, the ridges marched in scarlet and gold, summer birds wheeled in great flights and departed, brown leaves twirled sadly from the branches, far off at dawn or early evening could be heard the rutting bull snorting plaintively for his cow; days shortened, twilight began to fall early. Now it was high time to shoot a young moose, and to borrow from Mooin, the black bear, a winter rug, to set traps for mink, rat and otter along the brook, and in forest runs to hang cunning snares for foxes.

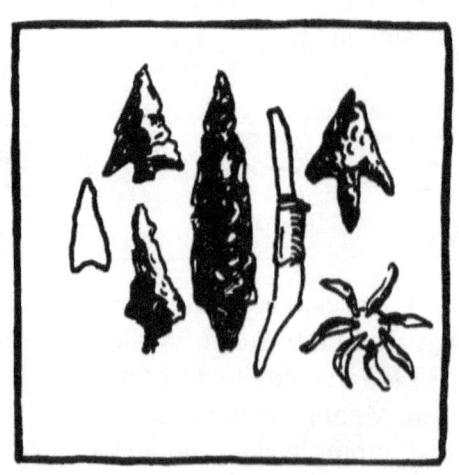

Canoe Builders

XIII CANOE BUILDERS

John Paul's second winter on the Rock was one of comparative ease. The weather was mild, the snows light, his stock of tobacco lasted well, and his store of corn, squash, potatoes, and beans guaranteed him against starvation. Seldom came the nightmare figures on the lake ice; he no longer watched so intently, for the clutching hand of the Law was almost forgotten. The Rock watched for him and he slept with greater ease, though never in the lodge but always on the Rock. True, he became impatient before the winter was over, and yearned for the coming of spring and the advent of Joe Meuse. Both came in due time; spring in early April and in May Joe, laden gunwale-deep. John Paul's store of fur, maple sugar, and ash wood had paid for all Joe had brought and left something for Mary. Again John asked no news of Mary and received none unsolicited. Nor did John Paul send any word to Mary, though he wanted her desperately. Perhaps a Micmac woman of the old time might have dwelt on the Rock with him, but not a woman like Mary who had seen fine things in white men's houses. Moreover, it would not be safe to take Mary away from the reserve; it might confirm the suspicion Joe Meuse had reported in Lawyer Freeman's mind. Again Joe departed, with laden canoe, promising to fetch tobacco plants if such things could be found. Again he was a man in a canoe, a flashing paddle, a speck lost in distance, nothing but rocks and mist.

It was in this second summer that John Paul decided to build himself a birchbark canoe. His canvas-covered canoe, that he had brought with him, was in good repair; Joe Meuse had brought him short copper tacks and white lead, and it would doubtless last for many years. But a canvas-covered canoe was after all a white man's contraption, easy to mend, it was true, after a rip on a rapid, but a soggy and wearisome load on a carry. Not so had his fathers made their canoes; theirs had been covered with tanned caribou hides, which were strong though heavy, but most frequently of the bark of the white canoe birch; these danced down a white-water like a pearl-colored bubble, a fleck of foam or a wind-driven leaf. A birchbark canoe, Skogumool, he should have as the old Micmacs had built them. Perhaps in October he would be obliged to go far afield to kill his winter's moose, and if so, he could bear his bark canoe lightly over the carries. Canvas canoes were but for those who could not run a whitewater without touching jagged rocks.

Manegwa, he cried gaily to himself as he set out one morning along the ridge to the place of great white birches. Half forgotten words of his childhood were coming back to him; manegwa, he remembered, meant to go on the hunt for the canoe birch. John Paul circled the glistening creamy trunks, slit them vertically, and cunningly peeled oblong sheets free from knot or blemish. How good the fresh bark felt to his touch, how sweet was the scent of new peeled birch! It took him all day to select just the sheets he wanted; Skogumool must be flawless and perfect; and it was evening before he returned to the brook bank with the gleaming load upon his shoulders. He eased his load to the ground, and walking swiftly to the Rock, looked up and down the lake. He had been absent all day long, and was more careless in watching now, since he felt the Rock watched for him.

"I build Skogumool, Great Rock."

"Good! Your fathers before you built of the gleaming bark."

"I must go many days into the forest to fetch straight and bending wood for keel, ribs, timbers, thwarts and gunwales."

"Good! I will watch; I see all that moves on the lake; neither Kwemoo the loon, nor Tamagune the shelldrake escapes my eye."

On many following days, John Paul split and carried the wood for his canoe. Keel, ribs, timbers, and gunwales humped amidships, after the old Micmac fashion, were of tough but easy-bending spruce; the thwarts of stout ash; stem, sternpost, and paddles of bird's-eye maple. To build the canoe was a labour of love, not a dull task like the digging and planting of his garden, which he had just accomplished; this work took cunning and skill of hand.

When John fitted the ribs, pounding the ends beneath the gunwale, he made a hollow drumming sound that was sweet to his ears. One day, when he was engaged in this particular work, pounding, grunting, and sweating in the August sun, he heard Pulowech, the partridge, drumming his wings in some sunny dusthole he had scratched out. John dropped his wooden mallet and laughed aloud; the sound that he made in tapping the hollow canoe with his mallet and the sound of Pulowech's drumming wings were the same. Now he suddenly knew why the old Micmacs had called Pulowech, the partridge, the canoe builder. John picked up his mallet and went on with his work, recalling as he worked the merry tale of Pulowech, the partridge, heard in his childhood.

Many times as he tapped on his hollow canoe, he repeated this tale to himself and told it to his Rock as he smoked his great pipe at night.

N'karnayoo, in the old time, Pulowech, the partridge, had been the canoe builder for all the birds. Yes, he was a mighty builder, and hence all the feathered folk called him Mitichihess, and held him in great reverence. Now Pulowech became full of vanity and put on airs, and was so conceited that he promised canoes for all the birds on a certain day, and hinted that his own canoe would far surpass any. Yes, he would build canoes for all the birds at once. And on the appointed day, the birds came together to claim their craft. Sure enough, Pulowech had them all ready. The eagle paddled off in his, using the tips of his wings for paddles, and screaming with delight; after him went Ko-ko-kas, the owl, paddling in like fashion; the crane followed; then the bluebird, the snipe, the impudent blackbird, all paddling proudly their glistening canoes of white bark. Last of all came A-la-mussit, the humming bird, in a tiny bark hardly larger than half an eggshell; for him Pulowech had made a paddle of maple wood, scarcely an inch long. "Look," screamed Ishmegwess, the fish hawk, soaring in the blue, "look, a squadron of canoes is coming on the lake."

Then after their first excitement was over, the birds were surprised that Pulowech had built no canoe for himself; but when they questioned him, he shook his head, looked important and mysterious, strutted to and fro on the lake shore, drumming his wings and hinting that he would build for himself the most wonderful canoe in all the world. "Come when the next moon is full," he said proudly, "and you shall see Pulowech's canoe."

At last Pulowech's canoe was finished, and on the day appointed all the feathered folk came to the launching. Now Pulowech had reasoned, that if a canoe having two ends could be paddled in two opposite directions without changing the course, a canoe which had many ends could be paddled in many directions. So he made his own canoe round like a nest, with no ends, yet infinite ends. The birds stood respectfully upon the shore, the wondrous canoe was launched, off floated old Pulowech, the wise partridge, proudly twirling his paddle of maple wood. But when he dipped paddle in water, the canoe twirled round and round and went in no direction. Pulowech paddled fiercely and only swirled in a foaming eddy. Then the birds began to laugh, each in his own fashion; A-la-mussit the humming bird twittered in the air, Ko-ko-kas the owl grinned solemnly behind his wing, the knees of Kosqu' the crane were weak and bent beneath him, Tjidge-is-skwess the shameless snipe rolled in the mud, bluebird and blackbird were downright impudent and saucy, the eagle screamed with merriment. Then Pulowech, the partridge, was so ashamed, and so chagrined after all the airs he had given himself, that he left his canoe in mid-stream, and flying far inland, hid himself in thick bushes, where he remains to this day. And although he still drums like a canoe-maker, he avoids all lakes and rivers.

With this tale of Pulowech, and many other merry tales, John Paul amused himself as he hammered in the sun. As he built, he was astonished to find how many strange names he knew for different parts of a canoe, or things that concerned a canoe. He remembered that an old Indian had told him that there were over seventy such Micmac words; little by little, many of these came to him: ĕdoole,—to build a canoe, tĕlooska—to go for timbers, nĕmjesemoonŭl and okwojegun—thwarts and gunwale, boon—the sitting place, and boonaak—the ribs of the sitting place, elamkaam—to prepare the ship yard, ootaagun—a paddle, pegoogwodum—to pitch the canoe, sigunbaadoo—to fill the canoe with water to test for leaks, cheema— to paddle, ootubeck—tough, fibrous roots for sewing the bark together.

When the canoe was completed, pitched, gummed, and tight, John Paul was pleased with the work of his hands, and looked at her with eyes full of admiration as she lay in her cradle. Never, it seemed to him, had he seen so splendid a canoe. Her creamy bark was without flaw or blemish, her gunwales sank from bow to stern in graceful sheer to rise amidships in the Micmac hump, the broad beam and rounded bilge at the amidships waterline melted by easy curves to nothing at stem and sternpost; no piece of faulty wood had gone into her; her seams were all sewn evenly with the fibrous roots of the spruce tree, and tarred in straight lines with the gum and resin of the pine tree; her gunwales and thwarts were stained crimson with the juice of the alder root, her paddles yellowed with golden thread. Then with infinite care on stem and sternpost, John Paul carved little figures like these from the Micmac sign language. The priests said these signs meant three divine persons, but John Paul knew better; they represented Glooscap, his grandmother, and Martin; and John carved them as a tribute to Glooscap the gracious giver.

At last one day he launched his canoe into the brook, and guided her down the run toward the lake. She floated light, responding to the slightest touch of his paddle. He would show the Rock his work. He paddled out into the lake, turned eastward and paraded up and down, flashing his paddle in approved Micmac fashion, and speeding Skogumool through the waves.

"Is she not good?" shouted John Paul.

The Rock nodded approval.

"Is she not in the old Micmac style?"

"She is like what your fathers built in the old time."

"Nothing of white men in her?"

"She is n'karnayoo, of old time, before whites came."

"Does she not ride the lake waves well, and yield quickly to the paddle?"

"She is as graceful as a young naked Micmac girl, she rides lightly as Kwemoo the loon, and flies straight as an arrow from a well-strung ash bow."

With this approval of his Rock, who had seen canoes from the beginning, John Paul was proud and happy, as he paddled upstream to hide his canoe near her building place.

Wind-Bird and Beaver

Days of week and month were for John Paul long forgotten; only the change from cold to heat, from heat to cold, the waxing or waning moon, fresh foliage or falling leaf, the coming or departure of birds, marked off the seasons. Save for the tobacco Joe Meuse brought each spring, his advent was hardly necessary to John Paul's existence. He measured his life no longer by clocks and the passing of time, but by natural events, that seemed great to him.

In September of his third year near the time of the autumnal equinox, came the great gale, that lasting through a whole day and night, lashed the lake into foam, tore furiously at his Rock, and laid hundreds of great trees in the forest. Black ragged clouds drifted across the sky, blinding rain beat at him, the thunder horses galloped out of the south, jagged lances of fire rent the clouds, and in the intervals of rumbling and explosive thunder, the wind shrieked and yelled like a thousand hungry Chenoos. Away went his canvas cover in an angry blast to disappear above the tree tops; he had to bale his watchtower as if it had been a boat on the sea. It was impossible to stir abroad to do aught, and for once he abandoned his watchtower, and clutching rifle, cartridges, tobacco and pipe, ran for the shelter of his lodge. In passing, he noticed that his ripe garden corn was flat to the ground. Among the thick spruces of the forest the wind could not tear at him. It was needless to watch from the tower, for no soul could live on the lake in such a gale.

John knew what was the matter, and when the weather had cleared, he returned to his watchtower and told the Rock about it. It was not that Muntu or Glooscap was angry; no, it was because the malicious wind-bird had loosed its wings again, and was flapping madly. Glooscap would soon set that to rights.

N'karnayoo, in the old time, he told the Rock, Glooscap had gone out upon the Bay to hunt wild fowl, and so strong a wind had arisen that his canoe was well-nigh overset, and many Indian canoes upon the beach were broken by the great waves the gale raised. Glooscap knew that the wind-bird had done this, so he set out to the far north to find him. Many days he travelled, till in the regions of ice and snow, he found upon a high rock, Wachowsen the wind-bird, the wind-blower, great of form and white as driven snow.

"Grandfather," said Glooscap to him in a friendly tone, "you blow too hard, you do great harm to my children. You break their canoes, and they can neither hunt nor fish."

"From ancient times I have been here," answered the solemn and arrogant wind-bird; "before the first voice spoke I moved my wings, and I will ever move them as I will, for I am above all power."

Then in anger, Glooscap towered high as the clouds, and in both hands seized Wachowsen as if he were a wild duck, lashed down both his wings with thongs of tough moose-hide, and cast him into a deep cleft in the rocks. Then Glooscap returned to his people.

Now came day after day of calm weather, so that the Indians could paddle forth to hunt and fish at all times; never a breeze stirred the surface of sea, lake, or river. Then after a while, upon the surface of all the waters, came a scum that was stagnant and stank. No longer could the Indians with their flares see Pulamoo, the salmon, rubbing his belly against the gravel of river bottoms; indeed the noxious scum became so thick that they could scarcely paddle their canoes through it.

"Ah," sighed Glooscap to himself, "I have done my work too well."

Again he travelled north and found the wind-bird, who is immortal, lying in the deep rock cleft where he had thrown him. He lifted him out, set him upon a rock, and loosed the thongs so that he could flap one of his wings gently. Then came moderate breezes that drove off the scum from lake and bay, and since that time the winds have blown favourably for Glooscap's Indians.

"Now," said John Paul, as he told this tale to the Rock, after the days of the great wind, "that rascally Wachowsen has perhaps worked his other wing loose, and Glooscap will have to attend to him again."

In his fourth summer, John Paul had another curious adventure. That spring he had planted and weeded his garden with great care; then for two or three weeks he had left it unvisited. He had been busy about something, though sometimes he did this by design, so that he might mark with pleasure how much his plants had grown in his absence. On his return to his garden he found, to his dismay, the bottom land under four inches of water, and all his lowland plants destroyed. It was well that he had sown the major part of his plants on the gently sloping hillside. John Paul was amazed; there had been no heavy rains for days. He waded down to the brook bank; the whole brook was backed up into a still-water that overflowed its level banks.

An amazing and startling phenomenon, that gave him a catch in the throat and made his heart beat faster. The lower run was dammed, but who could have built a dam without his knowledge, and why had such a dam been built? Cautiously, with his rifle at the ready, he parted the alders and crept along the brook bank, snapping never a twig. When he came to the swift narrow run above the outlet to the lake, he found the cause and uttered a few Micmac curses. There was a dam right enough, and one glance at the gnawed poplars told John Paul who was the builder. It was Qwahbeet, the beaver, a rogue always unfriendly to Glooscap and the Indians.

Sometimes, within the past few weeks, a colony of beavers had migrated, and deciding on some upper stillwater bank as a suitable summer home, had built their houses with subaqueous openings along the swampy banks, and had dammed the narrows to keep the water well above their front door entrances.

"Hell a damn!" thought John Paul; "beavers are stubborn beasts, and till winter I will have little chance to trap or shoot them."

He waded thigh-deep into the stream to inspect their work; it was well done. The beavers had cut hundreds of young trees, for the most part poplars and white birches, three or four inches through the butt, floated and towed these downstream, and having stuck the butts an amazing distance into the mud of the bank, let top and branches point upstream to catch all the debris and flotage of the brook.

John began patiently to break the dam by untangling tops and branches, pulling out deep-stuck butts, and casting the small trees out upon the bank. As the channel opened, down came the pent-up water in a rush that well nigh carried him off his feet. For hours he tugged and strained, pulling out trees and throwing them clear, till the channel was open and the brook began to approach its normal height.

But in the night the beavers repaired their work, cut more trees and built the dam so high that by morning his interval garden was under deeper water than before. Again John Paul laboured to tear down the dam; again the beavers rebuilt it. All through the summer the battle was waged, and in the end the beavers won, and the bottom land of John's garden was completely drowned.

Many a palaver had John Paul with the Rock about his enemies the beavers, and it was on the occasion of this struggle that the Rock first told him an ancient story. At least, it seemed to John Paul that the Rock told him this story.

"N'karnayoo, in the old time," began the Rock, in John's deep voice, "Qwahbeet the beaver was ever unfriendly to Glooscap and the Indians. Once Glooscap had chased the Great Beaver from Fairy Holes in northern Cape Breton down through the Bras-d'or lakes to Wycogamagh. There he had killed that beaver but a still greater one had sprung up in a nearby swamp. At him Glooscap had flung a great stone that missed the beaver but landed in little Bras-d'or, and made what the whites called Soldier's Island. Down the St. Peter's river went the beaver with Glooscap at his heels, and so many turns and twists did the fleeing beast take that he made the St. Peter's River channel full of short winding curves as it is to this day.

"All the way to the Bay of Fundy Glooscap pursued the Great Beaver, who hid somewhere in the rocks of Blomidon. Then with one scoop of his paddle, Glooscap in his anger scooped out the Basin of Minas, and entering, caught and killed the beaver somewhere near Cape Split. Here you can still see the Great Beaver's ribs embedded in the stone. That," added the Rock, "was just before Glooscap crossed to Pictou to say good-bye to the Micmacs, when he and his grandmother and Martin were setting off for the far north. He told the Indians at that time that he had settled their scores with Qwahbeet the great beaver."

John Paul shook his head. In Glooscap's absence, he told the Rock, Qwahbeet was getting out of hand.

Then reverting to an earlier part of the story, he asked the Rock something about which he had often wondered.

"Do the whites understand the meaning of the word Pictou?"

"No," said the Rock, coming as near to smiling as a Rock can, "they understand nothing truly. Someone has told them that it means the bubbling up of air through water."

"And why, too, do some Indians bear that name?"

"They, too, are ignorant; through contact with white men they have forgotten their own tongue. None of the old Indians bore such a foolish name."

John Paul had his revenge when the snows of winter came, for he shot or trapped every beaver in that colony—fine winter pelts they had—and no more dams were built on his brook. Since he could not send these skins out by Joe Meuse—White Man's Law forbade the trapping of beaver, and even the tearing down of their dams, though they flooded mowing meadows—he made the skins into caps, coats, mittens, and warm soft rugs.

A Slim Indian Girl

John Paul was so busy through all these years, and found such comfort in his great friend the Rock, that he would have been quite comfortable had not sex hunger tormented him. Though he never asked Joe Meuse of Mary, when he came in the spring, he yearned for her. He yearned vainly for the sound of women's soft voices. In the spring when birds and beasts made love about him, in October when the bull-moose roared his wooing across the wooded ravine, and the cow answered with encouraging seductive grunt, he was half mad with love. Sometimes he stood on his Rock in the moonlight and prayed earnestly that Muntu would send him a graceful dark-eyed Indian girl from the forest. He listened intently; he heard the crack of a dried twig; his heart bounded, but it was only a vixen limping home to her mate.

One night as he lay in his rock nest, half mad with passion, he had a curious vision; he dreamed that he saw the mighty Glooscap making men by shooting arrows into the rough bark of an ash tree. Was that a sign, was that a message, an answer sent by Muntu to his entreaties? he asked himself.

Next day, he set about making a mighty bow of ash wood, which he strung with a thong of moose-hide. Long arrows he made, some of maple, some of Indian arrow, and that his arrows might be perfect and in the old style, he headed them with hard stone chipped from flinty fragments in the hills, and feathered them with long plumes from the fish-hawk.

Then eagerly he set out to find an ancient ash with crinkled lichened bark. Such he found on the edge of the great swamp. He waited till twilight was falling—that was the mystic hour—and prayed hard to Glooscap for a slim young Indian girl. Then he stood erect, bent the mighty bow, and stretched the bow-string to his ear. Twang, an arrow flew straight into the ash; twang followed its fellow. Now it was almost dark. As the sixth arrow sped on its course, and pierced the tree, John heard a strange noise like a muffled cry and saw something dark and swarthy slip from the ash bark. On the ground he threw bow and remaining arrows, and set off in swift pursuit. Something fled before him with strange whining cry; sometimes he was almost on it; sometimes it was fifty yards ahead. Sometimes he thought he caught a snatch of some old Indian song; sometimes a low mocking laugh was borne to his ears. All through the night he pursued; his skin was scratched by bushes, he tripped over windfalls, he stumbled into deep hollows. When he rose, the mocking laugh seemed ever in his ears. All without avail; the mirage was ever beyond him.

At daybreak he returned to his Rock—fatigued, hungry, bleeding and disconsolate. He ate a little, then flung himself down in the grasses at the Rock's base, to rest and sleep. He had given up the quest, for it had come to him in the forest, that not Glooscap, the gracious, but Lon, the devil, the mischief maker, had put the vision in his mind, to make a merry jest of him. Yes, Lon had done it; he worked no bodily harm upon men, but delighted in practical jokes and mischievous evil.

The Rock had apparently no great faith in women, for when John Paul consulted his wise friend on the advisability of seeking Mary in the reserve at Mooin River, the great Rock thundered, "No."

It was after this trying episode in John Paul's life, that he began to pick up lucky stones, stones with holes in them. It was dim in his memory, but now it came back to him, that these stones in which water had worn a hole had preserved the old Micmacs from much evil. After the merry jests that Lon had played upon him, he always kept a lucky stone upon his person, and piled many more about the rock shelves of his watchtower, to ward off evil dreams and Lon's m'teoulin, black magic.

Three Story Tellers

It was in a curious way that John Paul found the greatest of all his lucky stones, one that had a profound influence upon his life in the wilderness. It was in August of his sixth summer on the Rock that John Paul discovered that salmon were running up his brook, to spawn on the gravelly bottom of the upper pools and still-waters. They had found their way from the sea, across the great lake, and now for the first time in his years on the Rock, entered his brook. Here was a gift from gracious Glooscap.

About a mile and a half up the brook from his Rock was a red sandstone cliff down which a filmy mantle of white water flickered in the breeze, from the springs above. At the base of the red cliff the brook made a sharp angle and formed a long deep green pool. On the side of the brook, opposite the sandstone cliff, was a gravelly bar covered in times of flood, but dry in the summer season, an admirable place on which to land a fish.

Thither in the August of his discovery, John often repaired to enjoy the sport of hooking, playing, and landing the big fish, as in the days of his youth. He had brought a rod with him on his first flight, but when he looked it over it seemed a trashy thing, bought in a shop. He made himself a new rod of maple, the joints lashed together, and with a splendid butt ground out from the gnarl on the root of a sugar maple. He heated the broken handle of a fox trap in a fire of dried alder wood, and beat out a new sharp gaff, which he bound to a piece of straight ash. Line, gut, and reel he had brought with him and had preserved carefully. Flies he tied cunningly, using the feathers of hawk, bluejay, the red of the shelldrake, the yellow of wild canary. Fine flies he made, that were neither Black Dose nor Durham Ranger nor Silver Grey, but John Paul's specials, that were just as effective as those of Hardy Brothers in luring the sporting salmon from the gravelly depths.

One evening he stood on the bar, facing the red sandstone cliff. It was dusky in the ravine, for the sun could not penetrate there after four in the afternoon. He tied on a brown-bodied fly with a white and yellow hackle, and cast lightly into the sucking current, where the smooth tail of the pool was becoming a rapid. On his third cast, a big fish rose in a ridge of foam, and John Paul struck and hooked him firmly. Up the pool went the giant fish, the dripping line cutting the water. He jumped, he sulked and quivered, he turned over in the air, he lashed with his tail; in vain; line, gut, and hook held fast. John Paul gave him the butt and used the full strength of his maple rod. In twenty minutes the tired salmon showed his side, and John, working him to the brink of the gravelly bar, drove the gaff into his belly and lugged him kicking on the beach. But as he pulled out the gaff, the salmon gave a mighty flounder toward the water, and was almost back in the pool. John averted the disaster by dropping the gaff, throwing himself upon the fish, and working his left hand into the salmon's gills. Then easing his rod to the ground, he reached with his right hand for a stone, with which he tapped the salmon upon the head. That finished the struggle. But as John Paul lay panting upon the salmon, he saw something smooth, wet, and glittering upon the sand, that had been disturbed as he had pulled out the stone for the *coup de grace.* He reached out and put his hand upon it; it was a little image carved from hard stone.

The image was about five inches in height and dark grey in colour. John Paul knew somehow at first glance that it had been made by an old Micmac. The nose was large and prominent, the eyes large and close together, the lips flat yet full. All over the body were deeply incised lines, marking the breastbone, the ribs, the chest box. Down each leg ran a deep line; the arms were in one piece with the body, but the legs were separated from one another and the feet were most cunningly fashioned.

John carried the image home, gripped tight in his right hand, and next day chiselled out a niche in the wall of his rock nest, and set the image up near his shrine of grinding stones. The best of all his lucky stones, the image became in time his most treasured possession. Daily he looked at his image and often laid a flower in the shrine beside it, and at harvest time heaped the choicest of his fruits and vegetables around it. Here was a real link with the ancient past of his race. Some great medicine man had shaped the stone, and carried it on his person; perhaps generations of medicine men who loved Glooscap had handed it on one to another. Had it been lost, he wondered, in a struggle with a great salmon, such as he had had, and been buried deep in gravel? Many ages it may have lain there. He touched it with reverence; he had a visible God; now there were three: John Paul, the Image, and the Rock.

It was during the winter nights that followed the finding of

Ulnooktaoo, the Image, that John Paul did some thinking about religion. The bright stars blinked at him as he lay muffled in skins, beneath the moose skin that replaced the canvas cover carried off by the great gale. A charcoal fire glowed in the shrine and shone on the smooth surface of his lucky Image. He began to compare what he had learned from the priests with what he had heard from his fathers. The religion of white men made them sour, sad, and long-faced, nor did they practise what they preached. They said give, give, but they themselves gave only a little, after they had got much. Surely they did not think the Indians their equals before their God though they pretended to say so. They were too sad and solemn; John remembered how he and Joe had been sent from school for laughing at the story of Noah. Surely any man could see that that was but a merry jest. Some of the priests had been fat jolly fellows, it was true. He had liked the Mass, when Father Daucette came round; but then it was well known that Father Daucette's grandmother had been a Micmac woman. No, the gods of the Christians were hard, revengeful gods that locked you up in a burning Hell if you disobeyed their orders. But Glooscap had always been gracious and helpful to the Indians, and even the malicious Lon had been a merry god.

Jesus, the white man's God, was on the side of white man's law; the gods of the whites were perhaps suited to people who dwelt in towns and villages, but Muntu loved better the folk in deep forests and frozen wildernesses. How could the God of the whites understand an Indian's necessities? He knew nothing of hunting and fishing, of great hunger and strong cold. The priest had told them that in the sight of his God all men were equal; how could that be true? The whites never asked an Indian to their table, and even among the Indians some were better and stronger than others; one was the chief, some Indians excelled in hunting, some paddled a canoe more swiftly than others. Surely he had done no wrong, yet he would be punished by the white man's God. But Muntu understood; Muntu would deal fairly with him; he would ask to be tried before Muntu on the last great day. How was the Christian story of creation better than that of the old Micmacs? Was it better to be shaped of mud by a God's hand or nobler to spring from the ash bark, struck by the arrows of a hero?

One story the priest had told the Indians had impressed John Paul and stuck deep in his mind. This story he told to his lucky image, for he had often told it to the Rock before. Jesus had been a carpenter, a skilled worker in wood, and it was said that He made the best and easiest yokes for cattle in all the land of Palestine. His yokes never galled their necks, nor worked and scrubbed the hide from their shoulders. And from remote far-off parts, farmers had brought their oxen to the great yokemaker of Nazareth, to have cunning yokes made and fitted to the necks of their patient cattle. John Paul knew right well how rare a good yokemaker is, how clever he must be with hands and head, how understanding he must be, how patient with the oxen. This story he understood, and it gave him a real respect for the God of the Christians; he had to admit that no story of Muntu pleased him more.

Still, he told the Image, Glooscap had been a stronger and merrier God, who loved feats of strength and delighted in laughter and merry jests. When old Glooscap laughed you could hear him all the way from Chebogue to Cape North. He had always been on the side of the Indians, a guiding light to them in days of distress and trouble. In the early days, when the old Micmacs had crossed in big canoes from Cape Breton to Newfoundland, making their first stop for the night on St. Paul's Island, Glooscap had lighted fires on the black cliffs of Point au Basques, to guide their canoes through the murk of dawn. It was a great thing to have a God always on your side, and certainly the white men's God could never be on the side of the Indians. What did it matter? The Micmacs were dying or mixed with the French.

Will Glooscap ever come back, he asked his stone God, with his grandmother and Martin from the far north, where he had gone to make a vast armoury of flint arrowheads? How can flint arrows in the hands of a few Indians avail against rifles and great cannon? Ah, but perhaps sly old Glooscap is making magic arrows, that will fly in circles and pierce the breasts of a thousand men at one shot.

How grand it would be to have all the land again for hunting, to burn the silly towns and factories, to see the rivers clean again with no foul rotting sawdust and the salmon and sea-trout running freely in them, to have the green forest again clothing the land to the ocean's edge, to meet again at Tusket mouth in great fleets of canoes, where the Micmac fathers used solemnly to confer on the distribution of districts for hunting and trapping rights. How grand to be free again and never see a white face!

"Will Glooscap really come again?" he cried out to his Rock in anxious tones. There was no reply.

"Will Glooscap give me a sign some day?" he cried again.

"When you feel a great shaking of the ground, when the rocks are upheaved, when the last great war is come, then Glooscap will give you a sign," replied John Paul in deep tones for the Rock, scarcely knowing that he spoke.

Now the winters were almost as cheerful as the summers, for there were three of them together: John Paul, the Rock, the lucky Image; and what grand lasting stories they told to one another. All about, it was so still and frosty that it seemed momentarily as if earth or lake ice would crack with a rending tear in the strong sullen cold. The charcoal fire in the shrine glowed dimly; the stars burned low and clear and seemed to give some sparks of heat to the frost-laden air. The three told each other stories of these heavenly points of light.

The Rock would begin with the story of the Great Bear. N'karnayoo, in the old time, the old men told many stories of the stars. The constellation of the stars which the whites call the dipper is really a big bear pursued by hunters. Megrez, Phecda, Dubhe and Merah make the bear; the handle stars Alioth, Mezar and Alcaid along with Arcturus and three others are the pursuing hunters. But the Rock called the stars by no such names as he told the story. The whites were wrong; the first hunter was the robin, Quipchowwech, the second, the chickadee, Chugegess, the third, the moose-bird, Mikchagogwech, the fourth, the pigeon, Pules, the fifth, the blue-jay, Wolowech, the sixth, Ko-ko-kas, the owl, the seventh, the saw-whet, Kopwech. Beside the second hunter was the companion star Alcor, but in his story the Rock called it Wo, the pot which the chickadee carried, in which to boil the flesh of the slaughtered Bear.

On early evenings of late winter or early spring, Corona Borealis, the Den, rode high in the sky with the mouth pointed downward. Then the Bear must crawl out of his Den or perforce be tumbled out. Round and round the pole-star began the chase; through spring and summer the hunters pursued the Bear and marked the hours of the night.

On, press the hunters; the little Chickadee with his heavy pot is placed between two of the larger birds to keep him in the trail, for what could the hunters do without a pot when they killed? One by one they weary as the lower stars merge into the mists of the northern horizon. First of all heavy Ko-ko-kas, the great owl, and the little owl, Ko-Ko-gwes, and Kopwech the saw-whet, lose the scent and drop out. But you must not laugh when you tell part of this story about

Kopwech losing his share of the meat, nor must you jestingly imitate his rasping cry, else he will shoot from the sky with a torch of blazing birch bark and set fire to your clothing and your wigwam. Next Bluejay and Pigeon lose the scent or grow weary of the hunting; only Robin, little Chickadee, lugging Wo, his pot, and the Moose-bird press on after their prey. In mid-autumn these three come up with the Bear, who at that season rears angrily upon his hind legs. Robin, the fearless one, pierces the Bear's breast with an arrow and over on his back he falls dead. The hunters are hungry after their long chase, but hungriest of all is Robin, who rushes forward so eagerly to secure a piece of the meat that he dabbles all his breast with red. As the hunters cut up the Bear with their knives, blood drips from the sky and in late September makes all the hard-wood ridges scarlet. The Chickadee lugs up his heavy pot, crams therein great chunks of bear's meat to boil, and sets the pot upon a fire. But the fat boils over and dripping down upon the earth makes the first snows of winter. Just as Robin and Chickadee begin to eat, up comes Moose-bird, who had lagged behind, screaming angrily and demanding his share. Hence the other birds call him behind his back Mikchagogwech, Mr. He-who-comes-in-at-the-last-moment. And to this day he appears at the last moment whenever a moose or bear is killed in the woods, screaming and demanding his share. Now when all the meat is stripped from the bones of the Bear, his spirit retires into the Den to sleep a long winter sleep till with the spring he is reawakened for a new chase round the pole.

Then in another tone, the lucky Image would tell the story of the Pleiades. N'karnayoo, in the old time, a man made love to his sister; that was accounted a great wickedness among the Micmacs. One should not sit alone in a wigwam with one's sister, nor speak to her, nor even look upon her. All that will bring nothing but evil and misfortune. But this young brave persisted in loving his sister and when she tried to escape, he pursued. She ran from the wigwam in the dead of winter, her brother at her heels. Crunch, crunch they went through the frosty snow of the forest; he was almost upon her, when pursued and pursuer came to the shore of a great lake. Out upon the ice she raced, he following swiftfooted. In mid-lake, he laid his hand upon her, but as he did so, the lake ice cracked and a great hole opened at their feet. Into this she sprang and sank in the black icy water. And after his sister dived the pursuing brother, deep as

Kwemoo the loon.

Now the other brothers of the wigwam had learned of this evil thing and set out after the two that fled and pursued. They followed the wide-spaced footsteps of the runners, the great prints of the man's moccasins, the little prints of the girl's, till the footprints vanished on the edge of the hole in the lake ice. They waited, and as the evil brother rose from the water after his deep dive, they speared him with a fish-spear and killed him. But to their amazement the sister rose from the hole as a great beautiful many-coloured bird, and dripping, fluttered into the sky, there to become the Pleiades and remind Indians for ever that it is an evil thing to make love to one's sister.

"N'karnayoo, in the old time," John would reply in his natural voice, "but do you know the story of the Morning Star, the glowing yellow ball that even now rises above the eastern spruces? That is a long tale but the best of all."

N'karnayoo, in the old time, once there was a family of Indian cannibals, the Cheenoos, eaters of human flesh, and among them lived a beautiful girl. The Cheenoos used her as a lure and she had to go out of the wigwam and wander about and invite strange young braves to come home with her. Then the mother would give them food from the pot and assign them a sleeping place on the blankets, but in the night the mother would arise and smite them on the head with an axe as they slept. Then the Cheenoo family would boil the flesh in a great pot and feast on it. But the beautiful Cheenoo girl, who was not a witch and flesh-eater like the others, hated this, and was sorry for the young men, especially when they were handsome and well-formed. Secretly she always threw away the share of flesh given her; she would eat none of it.

Once when her mother sent her out as a lure she met the handsomest of young Indian braves, who said to her smiling, "I go to your wigwam." He was tall, erect, and strong, with kind eyes, and his bright-coloured blanket hung carelessly from his shoulder. She loved him and faltered, "Do not come to my wigwam; great evil lies there for you." But he smiled and said, "I am stronger than evil, lead the way." She sorrowfully led the way to her mother's wigwam, for she did not know that the handsome stranger possessed powerful m'teeoulin, magic. Perhaps he was Glooscap, though the tale that the old men told never said so. The stranger entered the wigwam, but ate nothing from the pot, and presently lay down in the place assigned him. But he was watchful and did not sleep, for by magic he had read the thoughts of the Cheenoo mother. Presently, when all was quiet, he arose, and taking the beautiful girl by the hand, for he loved her, slipped out of the wigwam and fled with her through the forest. Now arose the old Cheenoo mother, fumbled in the darkness for her stone axe, and prepared to despatch the stranger. When she struck there was no crash of skull and bone but only a dull thud upon the blankets. Then she saw that the stranger's place was vacant, and a moment later observed that her beautiful daughter was also missing. Now the old Cheenoo woman was also possessed of powerful m'teeoulin; through the woods she ran screeching on the track of the lovers.

The lovers came to a broad open river with the Cheenoo witch just behind them. How should they cross quickly and escape! On the shore stood Tumwoligunech, the crane, dozing with head beneath wing. The handsome young brave went up to him and said: "What beautiful legs you have, Grandfather Crane." The crane half woke, pleased with the flattery, for the legs of the crane are always foul. "What a glorious neck you have, Grandfather Crane," went on the young brave. "Yes," said the crane, "my legs and neck are indeed fine though no one but myself has ever noticed them before. What do you want?"

"To cross the river. Stretch out your beautiful legs to either bank and we will use your back for a bridge." And the crane did so and they crossed safely and hurried on.

Then the pursuing Cheenoo mother came to the river and said to the crane: "Have you seen two running lovers?"

"Yes," said the crane.

"Set me across the river, dirty-legs, or I will twist your ugly wry neck," said the Cheenoo witch.

"Very well," said the crane, and he stretched his legs from bank to bank. When the Cheenoo mother was on his back, above mid-stream, however, he gave his legs a twist and off she fell into the swiftest of the current. That broke her magic, for after falling in water she had to return to her wigwam for fresh m'teeoulin. This she did, and tying on faster boots, she again pursued her daughter and lover.

These, meanwhile, fled till they came to the wigwam of a beautiful white-bearded old man. He was luminous and glistened like the canoe birch in the level morning sun.

"Good-morning, Grandfather," said the young brave. "We are

lovers fleeing from a Cheenoo witch. Help us."

The old man lifted up the bark at the back of the wigwam, and told them to slip out, hold straight on, and that they would be safe if they kept ahead till sunrise, for then the Cheenoos lose all their power.

"I will delay her," he said.

As the lovers slid out under the lifted bark, the witch-woman rapped upon the front entrance.

"Have you seen fleeing lovers?" shrieked the witch.

"I have," said the old man.

"Let me in," yelled the Cheenoo.

"Not now. Presently. I am dressing. Let me get on my clothes."

"Can I enter now?"

"Not yet, I am pulling my caribou shirt over my head."

"Can I come now?"

"Not yet, I am drawing on my leggings."

"Can I come now?"

"Not yet, I am tying my moccasin."

"Can I come now?"

"No, I have only one legging and one moccasin on."

Thus he delayed her, till the sun sprang out from the eastern pointed spruces, and the Cheenoo, with all her magic gone, fled howling.

Now the luminous old man, that shone like the chalk-white canoe birch, is the morning star, the old fellow rising now, and he stays always in the morning sky to make the world safe for lovers, till the sun comes.

Thus with many stories John Paul, the Rock and Ulnooktaoo beguiled away the long nights of winter. John Paul was happy in his friends; never had he had such friends; the Rock never slumbered but watched the lake night and day, the Image drove away Lon with his mischievous evil. Dreams and visions required interpretation, and who could tell him the meaning better than his friends. He examined the entrails of all beasts he killed, charred their bones in the fire, and read a story in the glowing embers. He set out upon no journey without advice and good counsel. He could see elves and fairies sometimes, and nightly listened to Mikumwess, the little men, forever busy in the deep hollows of the Rock. He had great respect for the Mikumwess, for they were made before men.

He almost dreaded the advent of Joe Meuse, who understood none of these things. Had it not been for the powder and caddy of tobacco he fetched yearly, John might have hinted that he had better stay away.

The Raid

Joe Meuse came faithfully in May for six springs, and while John Paul was grateful to his friend, he was astonished to find that each year he got further and further from his old friend. Joe Meuse had changed little; John Paul had changed much. The breach came from the fact that Joe Meuse understood little or nothing about John's new life and from John Paul's realization that Joe Meuse was not a true Indian but a white man's Indian, an Indian wearing white men's clothes and full of white men's thoughts and customs. This idea had been born in John Paul's mind on the occasion of Joe's third visit. They were sitting smoking in the shelter as they always did, when John Paul's eye fell and rested upon Joe Meuse's boots, boots made of cowhide tanned in a tannery, boots full of iron pegs and brass eyelets for lacing with shop-made laces. "White man's contraptions," he muttered to himself. No good in the woods, for they left a sharp heelprint, snapped a dried twig, and soaked in snow water. How much better the old Micmac moose-shank, that followed the form of the foot and helped you to slip noiselessly through the forest. John Paul hated Joe's boots.

In subsequent visits John Paul found fault with other portions of Joe's attire, with his coat, the castoff property of some white man, with the buttons upon his trousers, with the slouch hat made in some factory. Yes, Joe Meuse had upon him all the marks of a white man's Indian. In the old days before coming to the Rock, John had never felt this, for he too had been as Joe Meuse; but now that he had reverted to a primitive and simple state and had talked so much with his Rock and his Image, he hated all traces of civilization. In this he was of course unreasonable, for he himself had his gun, his axe, his files, and a dozen other products of the white man.

Joe Meuse, on the other hand, felt the coldness of his former friend. Did he not bring enough whiskey and tobacco? Did John think he had taken Mary? Here his conscience hurt him a little. Why was John more glum and silent each year, why did he look more and more like a wild man and mutter strange things? Perhaps John Paul was going off his head from living alone in the wilderness.

It was on the occasion of Joe Meuse's sixth and last visit, as they sat in the sun for dinner, that John tried Joe on a few words of the old Micmac. He tipped the frying pan, in which the fat sizzled, towards

Joe Meuse and said "Pŭtow." Joe stared at him blankly. "Pŭtow," John Paul repeated, shaking the pan, with no gleam of understanding or response from Joe. Joe did not remember the simple word Pŭtow, gravy, and yet Joe Meuse had heard as much Micmac as John Paul, when a child. A little later John Paul held out the pan again and said, "Maibeäsĭgŭn," meaning bacon; but Joe Meuse only smiled vaguely without understanding or response. Yes, Joe was hopeless; he had forgotten the customs and language of his fathers. After Joe's departure John Paul consulted the Rock and the Image in regard to this matter and they both confirmed his opinion.

In May of his seventh spring upon the Rock, Joe Meuse did not come with deep-laden canoe. John watched for him daily and was by turns pleased and disappointed by his absence. Though coldness had grown between them, he had never realized till now how much he depended on Joe's coming in the spring. Joe told him nothing, yet Joe was his link with the outside world of men. Through June he watched, perturbed and restless; he could settle down to nothing. What had happened to Joe Meuse? Was he dead? Now that his garden was established and his seed saved from year to year, there was no danger of starvation; but he had been lavish with tobacco and his store was low. Through later June he watched by day and night; Joe did not come. His tobacco was gone and he sickened of the taste of dried willow bark. Surely Joe would come with tobacco. Sometimes he fancied he saw a speck far down the lake, and his heart bounded in his chest, but it was only Kwemoo the loon rising from the depths. He watched, lifting imploring hands to Glooscap. Joe did not come.

In despair he consulted the Rock. "Joe Meuse does not come. How shall I get tobacco, old friend?" And after a long pause the Rock replied, "Are there not stores of white men beyond the hills? Your fathers knew how to raid slyly."

So in late June John Paul was absent from his Rock for six whole days, and one night parted the bushes to stare down at the roofs and chimneys of a village that lay in the bottomland, in the elbow of a river. He stared till after midnight. The yellow spots of light winked out. Then he ventured slyly along lanes among the homes of men.

Next morning the raided village was astir with a mystery. The wood of the grocery store window had been cunningly cut through, the glass lights removed, and the store entered. Safe-crackers from the States, beyond a doubt. Two caddies of tobacco and boxes of cigars and cigarettes were missing, and upon the counter were piled pelts of five mink and otter, worth thrice the value of the stolen goods. Wise rustics wagged their beards and made wild guesses, but the village schoolmaster, who wrote for the county paper, made much of the incident in his column. It passed almost unnoticed in the whirl of excitement then shaking the world, but a grey-headed lawyer in Mooin River clipped that item from the county paper and laid it in the drawer of his desk.

John returned to his watchtower triumphant. He was a raider now, a true Micmac, and he boasted much of his exploit to Ulnooktaoo and the Rock, and laid cigars, cigarettes, and a fig of tobacco upon the shrine. He laughed at the cigarettes of the foolish whites; that was a child's smoke, but they were light to carry, and though he had stolen them in way of jest, they might serve.

August faded into September with no sign of Joe Meuse. John kept a watchful eye upon the lake and tried to hope that Joe would never come again. He would live ever alone; he needed no white man or white man's Indian. He could repeat his recent venture and through many winters he and the Rock and Ulnooktaoo would tell each other many stories.

He busied himself in making a caribou coat such as the old Micmacs had worn. When it was neatly sewn and quite finished, John took the red juice of alder and stained the seams red within and without. He would do all as the old Micmacs had done. Now that Joe Meuse came no more, he felt gladly that he was completely severed from white civilization. Willingly, though perhaps unconsciously, he reverted more and more to type. One night he painted rings of red and yellow about his ankles and long strips of red from thigh to knee. Half in jest he began to practice the scream, that dreadful yell, that had been a painfully acquired art among the early Indians and had brought midnight terror and dismay to many a sleeping village. The Rock and Ulnooktaoo nodded approval. Surely he was safe and forgotten now; the restless white world would touch him no more.

The Betrayers

An angry crimson sunset upon the whole earth darkened to a sullen twilight; in the north the wind-blower puffed his swollen cheeks and the summer leaves fled in shuddering armies; in the sky the Thunderer blasted out cloud fortresses, darted swift golden lances, and from his brazen rattling chariot goaded to madness his galloping horses; under the earth the Earthshaker rumbled and groaned in the bowels of the earth, straining its ribs and solid shell. The war of the nations that Glooscap had told of so often was come. Kings and emperors opened the chess board of Europe, and took pawns from the ends of the world. "Tarantara," sang the bugles; "tarantara," echoed the silver cavalry trumpets; the military bands began to play; war madness grew in the minds of the peoples; the rail-thronged transports warped out into the stream; in the cold north, in steaming jungles, men, the most combative of animals, killed one another for causes neither cared for nor understood.

How could the world's turmoil and confusion reach into the wilderness and touch John Paul, who had renounced the world of men, who busied himself with simple duties, and spent his leisure hours in telling the Rock and Ulnooktaoo stories of the old time heard from his fathers and embroidered by his rich imagination? But the world confusion did touch John Paul, for just as a stone flung by a careless hand into a calm pond may make a ripple that breaks the slender reed on the far-off margin, so, in our world of curiously interwoven human relationships, the impetuous decision of some man in high place may mar or break some simple soul in a remote and hidden corner of the world.

When the Great War came in August, 1914, the village of Mooin River became a fever spot of patriotism. The tribal spirit is strong in the hearts of men just emerging from barbarism; the scratched surface reveals the savage; the stranger is still an enemy, the circle of fear only a little wider than in the days of the cave man. Old men made fiery speeches in hall or village street; young men, in whose hearts burned the love of adventure, rushed to arms. Lawyer Freeman, because he was the chief man of the district, and because of his fiery patriotism, was appointed chief recruiting officer not only of Mooin River but of the whole county. David, tall golden-haired boy, light of his father's eyes, left the university to join up with the first division.

When David was torn and killed by a shell in an early clash with the enemy before Ypres, the grey-haired father became a fanatic in the service of the army, combing the countryside, driving through drifted snow to speak to farmers' boys in little schoolhouses, in his search for the strongest young men to fill the ranks of the second division.

Joe Meuse was very unhappy about the war; all of the young Indians, save himself, had been pressed into the service; he alone, for no reason that he could name, hung back. Lawyer Freeman looked at him with eyes that blazed scorn; some of the shopkeepers refused to sell him tobacco; one night as he passed along the village street a group of boys at bridge-head flung "coward" at him from the darkness. That word stuck in his heart like a twisted arrow. He was no more afraid than the others, but how could he forsake John Paul on the Rock? He knew not what to do nor where to turn. He dared not join John Paul on the Rock since both would then be cut off, nor could he get any word to John Paul through the forest snow of winter. The climax of misfortune came for Joe Meuse when a group of recruits seized him on the village street, bound his hands behind him, and sewed white feathers on his coat. Back to the reserve he tramped, a patent object of scorn and reproach.

Winter melted into spring. Joe the stoic, almost beaten, began to overhaul his canoe for the journey to his friend. He had been able to buy nothing in Mooin River, but he had tramped weary miles to Digby for a caddy of tobacco and carried it home upon his shoulder. He scraped and painted his canoe and left her ready for launching at the upper stillwater. Next morning when he went to make further preparations for departure, he found that someone had taken an axe and smashed his canoe. Canvas was torn into strips, ribs, timbers, gunwales chopped into kindling wood. Joe stood viewing the wreck in despair; now he could not go to John Paul. They had beaten him, he must enlist for the war.

In his despair, he turned to Mary, and that night told her the secret of John Paul's hiding place, of his broken canoe, of the insults he had borne, and that he must now leave John Paul and go to the war. He was angry with himself the moment John Paul's secret had escaped him, for while Mary had known that for six years he had visited John Paul, Joe had never before revealed the secret of his hiding place. The world of men was against him; now that he was going far away, he had to lay bare his heart to someone, and to whom else but Mary?

"Wait some days," she said to Joe Meuse as he departed, "let Mary think."

Now Mary was tired of living alone—of what good was a man who dwelt on a Rock in the wilderness, and must always dwell there?—and for a long time she had set her heart upon Joe Meuse. Long ago she had loved John Paul, but now she feared him, for she could never drive from her mind that dreadful night in the cabin, with the crimson stain upon the sanded floor. With the years the conviction had grown in her mind, that she must never see John Paul again; she could not endure his searching eyes.

Joe Meuse was already doomed though he knew it not, for great is the power of a woman when a man's heart is low. For some weeks she kept Joe Meuse waiting as she thought out her plans, and in these weeks he was with her daily, since he could seek comfort nowhere else.

One night of early summer he felt he could endure his situation no longer. He would have attempted a long weary journey to John Paul on foot had he not been fearful of being tracked and followed, for he feared a greater surveillance than really existed. He could bear scorn no longer, he would go to the war with the others.

"I go to war, Mary," he said on entering.

"Don't go, don't go, Joe Meuse," pleaded Mary, going to him and putting her shapely arms on his shoulders. "Don't go, Joe Meuse! Stay with me and be my man."

"John Paul your man," replied Joe, flattered in spite of himself, for Mary was the most comely of all the Micmac women.

"What good man on Rock? Me want you, Joe Meuse; me afraid John Paul; me love you, Joe Meuse."

"Come to say, Mary, me go to war; ask you to take word somehow John Paul when summer come hot."

"How can squaw paddle so far, how carry canoe over long portage?"

Joe Meuse was nonplussed from the start; no woman could go there alone, no former friend trusted to go with her.

"Don't go war, Joe Meuse. Go with me."

"John Paul, he starve maybe."

"John Paul got beans, corn, potato, plenty moose, rabbit, partridge, in forest. John Paul no starve." Mary had a dreadful memory of John Paul's resourcefulness.

"No tobac there; bad when Indian got no tobac in forest. John Paul find us, kill us sure," said poor Joe, weakening.

"No, go to Malecite friend in deep woods on Miramachi waters where John Paul never come."

"Can no leave John Paul alone on rock always, Mary. Go to him after war?"

"Why no leave John Paul? You say he heart friend no more. Me fear John Paul; come go with me, leave war and see John Paul no more."

"How travel Miramachi, no money for iron train, iron boat."

"I get much money. Lawyer Freeman owe me and promise pay soon. Tomorrow he pay."

"You no tell where John Paul is, Mary, you no tell."

"Me never tell," lied Mary briskly and went on, "You love me, Joe Meuse, be my man, go with me."

Joe still shook his head and demurred.

Then Mary flung him roughly from her. "Then me take Louis Toney or Sam Glode and go away with them. Go to foolish war, go get killed by white men laugh at you. You stay so long they call you coward when you come."

Joe Meuse surrendered at these last shots; if he lost Mary now he would have no one in the world.

"I go, Mary," he said humbly. With her strong arms about him and her body pressed close to his, he was a lost man.

Next morning betimes, Mary was at Lawyer Freeman's office and at his summons entered his private room.

"You say long ago you give hundred dollars when me tell where John Paul is."

"Yes," said the grey-haired man, with glittering eyes, "yes, and the promise holds good. Where is he?"

"Me know, me tell."

"Tell then," he thundered.

"Count hundred dollar first."

The old man drew a roll of bills from his pocket, counted them out and threw them on the table before him.

"Now tell me."

Mary gathered up her blood money and stuffed it in her pocket.

"You take canoe, upper Stillwater, paddle far, carry three times,

Mud Lake, Loon Lake, Crooked River, Round Pond, carry to Great Lake. You know him."

"I know Great Lake. Is he there?"

"It is far journey up Great Lake, when canoe point to sunrise, half way up lake on right hand side, a great heap gray stone."

"I know it, I know it. I saw it once. Is he there?"

"John Paul there."

"Does John Paul know what happened to Alan?"

"Know nothing, say nothing. Me tell where John Paul is, you give hundred dollars," and Mary turned and left the old man. As she walked homeward to the reserve she struggled with such conscience as she had. She wanted Joe Meuse; she was afraid of John Paul. She wished him no harm and she had heard white men say that a man could not be tried for murder if the body of the victim is unfound. She and Joe Meuse could travel by canoe up the great St. John and cross to Quebec waters where John Paul would never find them.

Next day Joe Meuse and Mary departed on the iron train, crossed Fundy Bay on the iron boat, and were seen no more in Mooin River. Their untold story is that of two fearful wanderers flitting from place to place, the shadow of John Paul ever upon them.

The Avenger

Lawyer Freeman sat long in his office after Mary had left him, his hands buried in his grey hair. He had waited a long time and he had won; soon he would know all and bring John Paul to justice. Strange that only yesterday he had clipped from the local paper the account of the strange robbery at Round Hill. John Paul had done that. Should he go alone or take friends with him, surround the Rock in the darkness, and wait for John Paul to break cover? David and Alan were children of his middle age and he was drawing on for seventy, but he was still strong, full of vigor, and straight as an arrow. There was no Indian that he could not take singlehanded.

And alone he went next morning, upon his shoulder the pack that in the old days he had carried so often in the company of John Paul and his boys. In the pack was a week's rations, a blanket, a waterproof sheet and his ancient blackened firepot. He knew how to live as the men of the forest lived. He carried neither rifle nor shotgun, but on his belt in a leathern holster, was little David's army revolver, that the colonel of the 25th had sent him from France. He left a note at his home saying that he would be absent for a week, but he told no one whither he was going. In his light single canoe he departed at dawn from the very landing that John Paul had left in terror years before.

June had been a month of heavy and unusual rains, and he paddled swiftly through swollen still-waters, and shortened carries by following flooded brooks as long as his canoe floated. He paddled fiercely and moved quickly by water, but the carries were slow and painful. The dim trails were swamps in the lowlands, and on the uplands running brooks rather than paths. Ankle-deep he struggled on with swaying legs; though the canoe was light, the amidship thwart cut cruelly into his neck, and when he took the burden on his head, the canoe seemed an intolerable weight. Over every carry a return journey must be made for the pack. Though he had snatched but a scanty breakfast and that before dawn, he stopped to eat no luncheon; every step brought him nearer to John Paul, his mortal enemy. Sometimes he thought that he would drop from weariness, but the flame of his spirit carried him on.

At night in the midst of the long portage, when he could stagger no farther, he laid up on a ridge of yellow birches, scraped the wet leaves from the ground, spread his rubber sheet, and built a fire at the foot of a giant trunk. He boiled his kettle, and drawing his blanket about his gaunt shoulders, crouched and stared into the blaze. He could eat and drink little after that day of weariness, but he could see many pictures of what seemed a meaningless life; he saw the faces of Alan and David, of the girl he had loved long ago, now a complaining invalid. John Paul's brown face smiled at him from a dying ember, and he scattered the fire with an oath and ground the coals beneath his heel. He must sleep; he must be at his best for the encounter. But no sleep came to close his restless eyes; all night he sat or crouched by the fire or rose to throw on fresh logs in a shower of sparks. It was deadly chill in the hour before dawn, and he drew the blanket closer about his shoulders and waited through time that seemed interminable.

With the first grey that glimmered on yellow boles, he was up and away, breakfastless, to paddle and carry with all the strength of body and spirit. By late afternoon of this second day of his journey, he had his canoe near the western shore of the Great Lake. He did not launch her nor step out upon the margin, for he knew of the loon's warning cry; instead he cautiously parted the branches of the thick alder belt and looked up the lake. He saw the far distant dim pyramid silhouetted against a grey-blue sky. So that was where John Paul lay hidden; that was John Paul's rock. He waited patiently; he would not launch his canoe till night fell, for he must take John Paul unawares.

Twilight deepened into the night, the lake water changed from deep blue to a black that accentuated the gleam of dancing white caps, as he pushed his light canoe into the Great Lake water. A chill wind pierced the marrow of his bones. What cared he; he paddled boldly, breasting the night wind; his fierce purpose bore him on. He hugged the southern wooded shore of the lake, for the watchful loons though silent were still abroad. With his goal in sight, he was no longer tired; he felt that he could paddle on thus for ever. About midnight a gibbous red moon rose and made a streak of crimson across black water and glinted on the canoe's wet side and gunwale. He kept close to the shore, but do what he could, the light touched him. Toward two in the morning he beached his canoe in the brook mouth, crept through the wood and up the slope as silent as a shadow, and stood erect and fearless at the foot of the Great Rock. For a long time he stood listening.

The Rock Speaks

John Paul, in his watchtower, tossed and groaned in uneasy slumber; far afield that day he had gone in quest of straight ash wood. Uneasy was his sleep, but heavy, so heavy that he but half woke when the Rock shuddered violently and Ulnooktaoo tottered from his niche and fell broken in halves among the stones of the shrine. Glooscap's prophecy was fulfilled; Kuhkw the earth-shaker, the mighty power who passes under the surface of the ground and makes all tremble with his strength, was at work. He half woke, and by habit rose on his elbow to look up and down the lake; the moon was rising, the wind chill, all quiet. He paid no heed to the Rock's warning, but lay down again and pulled the bearskin closer about his shoulders. He slept to dream of the liver-coloured giants, who, as soon as he threw them to earth, rose again refreshed; of Coolpujot, the boneless one, who, each spring and fall by the order of Glooscap, is turned over with hand spikes and lands with a mighty crash. He was in the brook again with the wicked frog and a floating black bear; he was drowning, he sat up gasping for breath—

"John Paul, John Paul!" someone was calling him.

He was but half awake, and he had heard so many voices in the night that at first he paid little heed.

"John Paul, John Paul, come down," called the voice again.

It was Joe Meuse. In his delight at hearing a human voice all his rancour against Joe, the white man's Indian, was forgotten. Joe Meuse had come again, and early, and had stolen on him unawares. Quickly he kicked clear of the fur bag, and leaving his rifle in the nest, slipped swiftly down the Rock's sloping side. As his feet touched the ground, a light was flashed in his face, and dazzled though he was, his quick eye made out the form of a white man, a flashlight in one hand, a pointed revolver in the other.

"I've got you now, Indian."

Swift thoughts raced through John Paul's brain: what a fool he had been to leave his rifle in the watchtower—that was worthy of a white man; not Joe's but Lawyer Freeman's voice; was he still dreaming? No, it was Lawyer Freeman right enough; the Law had got him at last; he could never escape that fearless old man.

"I've got you at last, Indian."

They must not take him alive; would it be best to close with the old man, or make a break for the forest? His hunter's instinct told him to try the second plan and involuntarily he moved his head to glance around.

"Don't move, Indian. You're surrounded." Surrounded, then it would be foolish to run, for they might wound him and bind him with ropes; better to close with the old man when they dared not shoot, and wrest the revolver and light from him. In the darkness he could scale the Rock and get his rifle and hold many men off. Slyly he shifted his left foot two inches toward Lawyer Freeman.

"I've got you now, Indian."

"Got me now, Mr. Freeman."

"What did you do with my boy Alan? Speak true, Indian."

"Me kill him," said John Paul simply, seeing no further use in concealment.

"Why, why in God's name, did you kill my boy?"

"He sport with Mary, my squaw. Come home sudden, catch them, burst door, awful mad, shoot Alan, throw him in river."

John gained an unseen inch with his right foot. "You lie, Indian."

"Me no lie."

"You lie, I say, and you're going to swing by the neck in the county jail for this. No Freeman ever ran with an Indian girl."

"Me no lie, Mr. Freeman." John Paul gained another two inches.

"Stand still, Indian." The old man stepped back a yard, and John Paul lost all the ground he had gained. "You think you can jump me, do you? Well, you can't, you're coming along with me when day breaks, and we'll hang you right enough."

"You no hang me, Mr. Freeman; no take me out alive; shoot me here maybe. John Paul done right; white man same when he mad and find man with wife. What you do, Mr. Freeman?"

"Shut up, Indian! Alan never touched your squaw."

"Why me kill him then?"

"Why, that's what I'd like to know," said the old man, his chin dropping for a moment on his breast. "But the fact remains that you killed him," he cried with suddenly glittering eyes. "But why, John Paul, why did you kill my boy?"

"Me tell true first time. Me no plan bad thing. Come on them sudden, shoot quick. Me always like you and boys, Mr. Freeman; little David like me. Me no lie in old time."

John Paul was fighting hard for his life, he had never spoken so much at any one time before. At the mention of David's name the old man's fire flared up once more.

"Yes, and the Huns have killed my little David. I've got no boys now, Indian, and by God, you'll pay for one and the Germans for the other."

In spite of his fierceness, there flashed across his mind a picture of John Paul with Alan and David at his heels on a bright day of spring on the Lac Joli Stillwater. There the Indian had taught them how to cast a fly and trail it cunningly in deep pools by the alder roots. But he crushed back those memories.

"Turn round and put your hands behind you, Indian, till I snap these on your wrists."

John Paul rested his right hand upon the great Rock for comfort. The swarthy Indian clad in rough skins and the tall white man with his shock of grey hair stood staring into one another's eyes. John Paul never knew whether he shouted or the Rock shouted for him.

"No, no bind John Paul. Shoot him here by the Rock. No bind him."

"You elect to die here, do you? Good, and I'll leave you here to rot in the sun. You're not surrounded, I'm alone. You'll be pleased to know that I'm shooting you with little David's revolver. Two minutes for your prayers, Indian," and he shifted the light for a second and glanced at his wrist watch.

"Who kill little David?" asked John Paul simply.

"The Germans, the Germans in the war."

"War?"

"Good God! don't you know the world's at war? Yes, they murdered little David, and you murdered Alan. I'll see to them later, just now I'm going to shoot you. A minute and a half, Indian. Say your prayers, say your prayers."

John Paul leaned hard against the great protector. He knew by the glint in the eye and the screaming voice that he was dealing with a man half mad.

"Help me, Great Rock, help me, Ulnooktaoo; help me, gracious Glooscap," muttered John Paul in a fervent prayer.

John Paul stood motionless. Dawn was beginning to glimmer on the lake; the wind had fallen; there was no stir among the great blocks of black clouds that chequered the western sky.

"Time up," shouted the old man, raising the revolver to shoot.

But with the very sound of his voice, flashlight and revolver dropped from his hands, and he fell in a crumpled heap before John Paul, overcome by hunger, exhaustion, and undue emotion.

Now was John Paul's chance to escape, or to end his quarrel with the Freeman family for ever. Such thoughts flashed through his mind, but the Rock, who knew that nothing escapes Destiny, told him otherwise. In his arms he gathered up the old man, scaled the Rock, wrapped him warm in furs, and laid him in the watchtower. He built a glowing fire of charcoal in the shrine, then slid down the Rock again to search for the old man's canoe. With ease he traced the footsteps through dewy grass to the brook mouth, and returning with the pack, poured some tinned soup into the camp kettle and set it above the glowing coals. He laid the revolver, that he had picked up on his return journey, upon a rock ledge and sat down to gaze at the unconscious man. He hoped Lawyer Freeman might not die, but he knew there was no escape from Fate. After two hours, he roused him, and forced him to drink a few spoonfuls of hot soup and a dash of whiskey, that John Paul had hoarded against an evil day. The sun came up in chill splendour, indifferent, as Nature always is to man's tragic moments. Through the livelong day John Paul sat pondering, rousing from time to time the man who had come with intent to kill, to give him meat and drink.

Towards four in the afternoon, the old man sat up and blinked his eyes, in which began to sparkle their accustomed fire. He fumbled at his belt and empty holster.

"John Paul, give me that revolver."

John Paul took it from the rock ledge and handed it to the sick man. His weak hands fumbled with it but presently broke it open; the six chambers were still full of loaded cartridges. Lawyer Freeman flung the weapon from him.

"You're no coward, John Paul."

"Maybe. Fraid Law."

"I suppose I ought to kill you, but how can I when you've saved my life? You had all the cards in your hand last night and today, John Paul. No one knew I came here."

"I guess that maybe. You no coward, too. Rock tell me, do you no harm."

"What rock? Rocks can't talk."

"Rocks talk same men maybe."

"I ought to kill you, for you killed my boy. But *cui bono,* who'll benefit by that? Something has put another thought in my head as I lay here. I believe now you spoke true."

"True, Mr. Freeman, just like happen."

"Many a white man, it's true, has got off on the unwritten law. But look here, you remember David?"

"Me never forget little David."

"Will you go to the war and avenge his death? Will you kill many Germans for him and me?"

"I go, Mr. Freeman, when I go free Law."

"Yes, you'll be free to go where you please after the war."

"Come back here, live with Rock; he best friend now."

"Come and go where you please, but in the war shoot many Germans for me."

"I go, I do what you say, Mr. Freeman. John Paul fear not bullets, but Law, hang, pen."

"Come then, let us start, there is not a day to lose," cried the old man, struggling to his feet. "Come, let us start at once."

"No," said John Paul, "no, Mr. Freeman, you too weak yet. John Paul many things to do about Rock. Early dawn we start."

The old man settled back in his furs and John Paul busied himself between Rock and lodge. There were many things to be hidden, many things to be greased, wrapped and stored away. Just as twilight was falling John Paul ran up the brook valley to have a last look at his garden. The rows were growing bravely, but no one would garner the crop that fall. Returning, he cooked a supper of brook trout for the old man, as he had done in the old days when he had been a guide. Chill night came with a multitude of burning stars; John Paul fed the fire with charcoal, smoked his pipe and stared up at the sky. No longer need he watch the lake, for Law was here beside him in the watchtower. Few words were spoken. Presently the white man and the Indian he had come to take or kill, lay down together in the snug nest, and pulled over them the blankets of furs. Each thought a little before sleep came; Lawyer Freeman of David far off in a muddy Flanders grave, John Paul of the wisdom and greatness of Glooscap and his gracious friend the Rock.

Both slept. The lake water lapped and played music of the old time among the reeds as the Great Rock cradled two poor human children. There was a melancholy sound in the forest; was it the sad night song of the brook, the rustle of restless poplar leaves, the moaning of some wounded wild thing, or was it the Great Rock sighing for all the weariness of ages past and the loneliness of years to come without the human babe it had loved and held for an instant?

Next morning they were off betimes. John Paul had risen, while it was still dark, and in the brook had washed all red alder stains from legs and ankles. He was going back to white men and must forget many things for a little. Everything that belonged to John's forest life was stowed away or hidden; the Rock stood bare as it had stood in the beginning. Amidships in his big canoe he piled many furs and made Lawyer Freeman sit there, though the old man protested violently and swore that he could swing a bow paddle. It was obvious to John Paul that the old man would do well if he staggered over the portages. They carried food for the journey, but so little dunnage that John could take both canoe and dunnage in one carry.

Halfway to the western shore, John turned towards the Rock, gaunt, bare, and lovely against the morning sky, and waved his paddle in farewell. Again when they reached the lower shore and beached their canoe in preparation for the first carry, John Paul parted the alders and stared up the lake for a long minute. He plunged his hand in his pocket, as he stood, and felt the broken halves of Ulnooktaoo. One friend would go with him to guard him against evil.

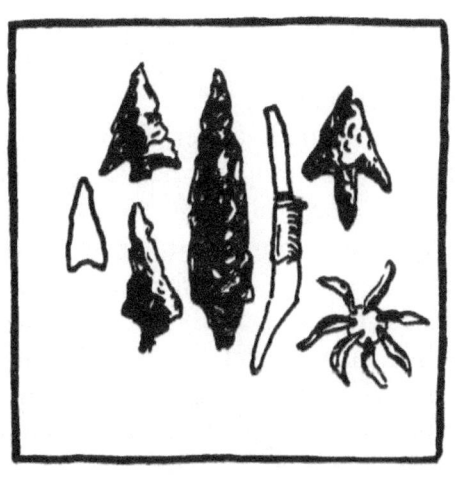

The Tribes at War

They made the journey through forest and stillwater quickly, and reached Mooin River in midmorning. John asked neither for Joe Meuse nor Mary. Lawyer Freeman kept him busy with enlistment papers and uniform, and by noon of the very day of his arrival in the village, he was on the train for Valcartier with a small draft. He knew none of his strange comrades and spoke to none. John Paul had never ridden on a train before, but he betrayed no astonishment. He kept glancing out of the windows for a first glimpse of the enemy, and wondered when they should arrive at the fighting place. This was a rash noisy way to approach an enemy, he thought, in a snorting whistling iron horse. What a story Glooscap would have made of all this. But that was white man's business, and he had given himself into their hands. Not so his fathers would have stolen on the sleeping villages. John Paul looked to his front, smoked his pipe and asked questions of no man.

After a two days' journey they reached Valcartier, a tented city on a wide plain, without any sight of the enemy. There John Paul learned that the war was not in Canada at all, but that far beyond the seas the English and French were fighting the Germans. But in the old days the English had always fought against the French. Well, it mattered not, he reflected; there must be some new treaty among the tribes. He was going to pay the score of his crime, and to avenge little David who long ago had said, "Wouldn't it be fine if John Paul were our brother?" He would keep his word and come back to the Rock when he had played his part.

He quickly made a good soldier, for by nature his carriage was erect and dignified. On the range he needed little teaching; he had an uncanny sense of distance, his eyes were good, and he had long known how to squeeze a trigger without pulling the muzzle down. With the stock of a Ross or Lee-Enfield pressed close to his shoulder, he was happy and at home. Quickly he learned to lob a bomb with accuracy and to dismantle and set up a machine gun with the requisite speed. Of his bayonet he was silently contemptuous, though he expressed no opinion, and the harsh army boots galled his feet, accustomed to soft moccasins.

So quickly did he learn, that within a month of his arrival in Valcartier, he was sent with the first draft en route to France through

England. The big transport astonished John Paul more than anything he had seen; she was as big, he reckoned, perhaps bigger than Glooscap's boat. Smiling he stood at the crowded rail with the others, though there was none to wave him good-bye, as the ship warped into the stream and a band on the pier blared out "The Girl I Left Behind Me."

His comrades paid little heed to John Paul; to them he was merely the big Indian, and no matter how low they were, they placed him in a lower social scale. He was very lonely in this crowded world of men. How melancholy was the ship's whistle, hooting a grim warning through the fog, how sad the sound of waves lapping against the ship's dark sides! On the first night out, when John Paul squatted on the murky deck, where no lights could be shown, no matches lit, a feeling of deep sadness came over him; he was being borne away from everything he knew and understood, to lands strange and men untried. His heart was very near his stiff army boots. Fate, he felt, had tossed him about through life. Of what use to be a faithful guide, to make good baskets and speak truth; those like Louis Toney who lied and made crooked baskets fared better. In his mood of sadness he thought of his great Rock standing firm, erect and true in the wilderness. Always the same, unchanging, proud, without lies— adviser, protector, a great friend. With the thought of the Rock much of John Paul's sadness vanished.

On subsequent nights, to further allay his sadness and banish his loneliness in a world of men who knew him not, John told himself merry tales of Glooscap. N'karnayoo, in the old time, said John Paul, though he knew these stories were not as ancient as the others, Glooscap himself had once crossed the seas, in a canoe perhaps bigger than this ship, for trees grew out of Glooscap's canoe. It was not the white men who had discovered America, but Glooscap who had discovered the Old World. That was a good joke on the whites. It had happened this way, N'karnayoo, in the old time:

Once there was a poor Indian woman, a woodchuck Moninkwess, who had lost her boy but who always kept thinking of him. One day a strange boy came to her and called her mother. She was glad, for he was a handsome shapely boy, though not her son. She pretended he was her son. The boy brought with him a magic pipe, which he gave to his new mother; when you blew on this pipe the beasts of the forest ran to you. One day the woman blew upon her pipe; a deer and qwahbeet, the beaver, ran to her wigwam. In the beaver's mouth was a stick. "Point this stick at any animal and though it be a mile off, it will fall dead." The woman pointed the stick at the deer; down it fell and the boy and his mother feasted on the flesh. Now the woman was no longer poor.

Then the boy, who was of course the hero Glooscap in disguise, began to build a great stone canoe.

"I go across the seas," he said to his mother.

"What will you do for sails?"

"Make them of leaves."

"Let the leaves alone," she said. "I will point my stick at many moose and caribou, tan their hides and make beautiful sails for you." And so she did. Glooscap stored the canoe with the dried meat, and killed many seals to make water-bags for his long journey.

He sailed straight for London with his mother. How the whites stared as he came up the river in his stone canoe to London town! They offered to trade a great warship for his stone canoe, but the crafty Glooscap said, "No," for he knew that a wooden ship might burn when he smoked his great pipe. The English heaped his canoe with presents and gave him an iron anchor and an English flag.

"Ho," said Glooscap, "now we will sail for France."

The French fired cannon balls at him all the afternoon, as he made the coast of France, but the balls bounced off Glooscap's ship of stone and did him no harm. Then by powerful m'teeoulin, Glooscap drew all the French fleet ashore. There they lay stranded in shallow water, their captains red-faced and cursing.

That night Glooscap laughed Ho! Ho! He held his sides, and the sound of his laughter ran from France to England.

The French took Glooscap prisoner, put him in a great cannon and fired it off. When they looked down the muzzle, there sat Glooscap laughing at them and smoking his stone pipe. When the King of France heard of this, he said, "I must see this mighty man," and sent for Glooscap to come to his palace. But Glooscap replied, "I came here to see no kings. If the King of France wants to see Glooscap, let him come to me." And the King of France came to Glooscap. Then to please the King, Glooscap took all the stranded men-of-war and drew them again into deep water. Then he sailed home with his mother to his own people. Yes, it was Glooscap, who had discovered the Old World, not the other way about, and it was only after Glooscap's visit that the whites began to cross the seas.

With such stories and thoughts of his Rock, through lonely nights, did John Paul drive black sadness from his heart as he crossed the dark sea. He did one other thing that comforted him; he drilled tiny holes in Ulnooktaoo and wired the broken halves snugly together.

Civilization

XXII CIVILIZATION

France, dirt, confusion, bursting shells, long marches, rats, stinks, lice, caves in the ground, wet muddy trenches. John Paul was in Company B of the 25th, the first Nova Scotia battalion. He bore all patiently, and was unafraid. He had a sovereign panacea against fear: when the enemy's barrage broke and men dived for dug-out or funkhole, he thought of his Rock, calm and majestic in the wilderness, a thing dauntless and unafraid.

He was soon selected as a sniper, and detailed to the scouts, for none could excel John Paul in stalking at night in No Man's Land. The scouts' officer learned to rely on his judgment and after a time made him a corporal. John looked with pride at the two stripes on his tunic's sleeve. Ah, that would be something fine to show his Rock. He was still silent and alone, the big Injun, to his comrades; though he never spoke unless spoken to, many leaned upon him in perilous times. He was a good soldier; so Captain Bill, as his men called him, noted him in his B company book. "Yes," Captain Bill would say, "John Paul is a *man,* some day he will be a sergeant."

Captain Bill was surprised at a number of letters he got from a man named Freeman in Mooin River, always asking: "How does John Paul do?" Once when he had time, he replied laconically: "John Paul is our best scout and sniper: he has twenty-two notches on his rifle's butt. Some day he will win his decoration."

Dawn came with full beauty on the morning of August 8, 1918. Larks rose from the meadows and sang as sweetly as if soaring o'er an English field. Little fluffy clouds were tinged with pink. Broken trees made a brave show of mid-summer foliage, that hid their torn branches. Wheat fields waved in their first yellow. Suddenly on the hills before Amiens, still in deep shadow, twinkled a thousand sparks, as if a sudden swarm of fireflies had sprung from earth. Two seconds later came a roar of Hell, as thousands of guns spat their venom upon the enemy. Tanks, cruel monsters of a mechanistic age, cast off their camouflage or waddled from the shelter of willows to lead the van. Amid smoke, dust and the mists of morning, in a hell of noise and flame, John Paul strode forward bravely with his comrades of the infantry. In front went the tanks flattening down mazes of wire, after them came the men of line regiments; behind, the guns bellowed. The 25th reached and occupied the enemies' front line; the barrage
106

lengthened; they advanced again; now they were in a field of yellow wheat, that reached well-nigh to their arm-pits. Suddenly John Paul felt a sharp blow upon his chest, and looking down saw that his tunic pocket was stained a dull crimson. He remembered with amusement having once seen a boy in the Indian school fall and break a bottle of red ink that was in his pocket. Then as if by magic, smoke, flame, noise and morning mist faded; stilled was the uproar of the guns. Whose heroic laughing figure was that striding from island to island? It was Glooscap. There before him in the calm of morning was the great lake bathed in sunshine, and there in its splendid setting of dark spruces and gay maples was his friend, his giant Rock upon the hill.

"Look," said Private Harris to Private Simpson, both of the Army Medical Corps, as in the twilight they rifled the pockets of the dead; "Look, mate, the big Injun 'ad a hidol in 'is pocket. Much good that done 'im." And he broke Ulnooktaoo and flung the pieces in the muck of a shell-hole.

John Paul's Rock

Ages ago a giant laccolith was thrust by plutonic forces into the folds of the hills from the boiling magma below. Ages ago it rode southward, its chariot a crystal mountain. Ages ago it drove its roots deep into the Nova Scotia hills. To it, a thousand years are as a day; man a new-comer. With the grey dignity of antiquity, it stands erect in a world of treachery, lies, strife and bloodshed. It will stand, long after the race of men has destroyed itself. Once, for a moment, it stopped to take a hand in a human tragedy and save a human soul. For a moment a man worshipped it as a God. When the south winds whine about it, when the north wind blusters up with blinding sleet, the Rock, indifferent to storm or sunshine, defies the weariness and loneliness of years to come. In the lodge nearby, still stand John Paul's tools and tubs that he had stored against his return.

His garden is a sad tangle of brambles. But the majestic cloud-capped Rock bears his name—Lawyer Freeman printed it in black letters upon the new white survey map—**JOHN PAUL'S ROCK.**

THE END
[40100 WORDS]